# DOCTOR WHO AND THE
# PLANET OF THE DALEKS

# DOCTOR WHO AND THE PLANET OF THE DALEKS

Based on the BBC television serial *Doctor Who and the Planet of the Daleks* by Terry Nation by arrangement with the British Broadcasting Corporation

## TERRANCE DICKS

TARGET

*published by*
The Paperback Division of
W. H. Allen & Co. Ltd

A Target book
Published by the Paperback Division of
W.H. Allen & Co. Ltd
A Howard & Wyndham Company
44 Hill Street, London W1X 8LB

First published simultaneously in Great Britain in 1976
by Tandem Publishing Ltd
and Allan Wingate (Publishers) Ltd

Reprinted 1978
Reprinted 1982

Printed in Great Britain by
Hunt Barnard Printing Ltd, Aylesbury, Bucks

ISBN 0 426 11252 0

# Contents

# I

# Jo Alone

The tall white-haired man lay still as death. The girl leaning over him could find no pulse, no beat from either of his hearts. His skin was icy cold to the touch.

She perched on the end of the couch and hid her face in her hands. All around her the machinery of the mysterious Space/Time craft called the TARDIS hummed gently and contentedly, as if unconcerned with its owner's fate. The column in the many-sided central console rose and fell. The TARDIS was in flight through the Space/Time Vortex.

The girl, who was very small and very pretty, rubbed her eyes and stood up. She opened a locker in the base of the control console and took out a small black box. It was very much like one of the tape-recorders common on Twentieth-Century Earth, although its power source was eternal and its recording capacity unlimited. This was the 'log' of the TARDIS, used only in emergencies. The girl switched it on and began to speak.

'My name is Jo Grant. For some time I've been the Doctor's assistant in UNIT—the United Nations Intelligence Taskforce. Recently the Doctor took me for a trip in the TARDIS. We travelled far into the future and became involved in a plot to cause a space war. The Doctor discovered his old enemy the Master involved in the plot—and behind the Master were the Daleks. Although the Doctor managed to defeat the Master and prevent the war, he was seriously wounded in a Dalek ambush. I managed to get him into the TARDIS.'

Jo's voice faltered as she remembered the dangers they had escaped. She steadied herself, and went on. 'The Doctor had a serious head-wound ... he was barely conscious. He managed to get the TARDIS to take off, then used something he called a telepathic circuit to send a message to his own people, the Time Lords. After that he started slipping into a coma. He said he might sleep for a very long time. He asked me to record what happened in this log.'

Jo switched off the log, and went to examine the Doctor again. When she'd finished she picked up the machine. 'The Doctor's breathing seems to have stopped. There is no pulse or heartbeat, and his skin is icy cold.'

Jo Grant paused, and took a deep breath. She was well aware that in any human being these symptoms could have meant only one thing—death. What gave her hope was her knowledge that the Doctor was *not* human. She had seen him in this kind of coma before; it had been part of the mysterious process by which his Time Lord body was able to heal itself after exceptional damage and stress. Jo hoped this was happening now. The alternative, that the Doctor was dead or dying, was too terrible to contemplate.

Suddenly she became aware that something was

8

happening. The sound of the TARDIS had altered. The central column was slowing down. On the control panel, lights flickered, switches and controls moved of their own accord. She switched on the recorder. 'The TARDIS seems to be landing—the Time Lords must be operating it by remote control. I hope they've brought us somewhere we can get help for the Doctor.'

She glanced at the Doctor again, then ran over to him in shock. His whole face was covered with a glistening white frost. Carefully, Jo wiped the frost from the Doctor's face with her handkerchief. For a moment she feared the Doctor really *was* dead. Then his eyes flicked open. They stared unseeingly at her for a moment, and closed again. Jo gasped with relief. 'Doctor ... oh Doctor, you're alive!' The Doctor gave no sign that he had heard her. He seemed to have sunk back into his coma.

Jo became aware of a squelching, slapping sound. It was coming from *outside* the TARDIS. She went to the control console and after some fumbling managed to find the scanner switch. Slowly, a dim picture appeared on the little screen.

It showed a stretch of dense jungle, vines, trees, creepers and strangely shaped plants jostling each other for room. She knew at once she was not on Earth. The vegetation was alien, with a sinister fleshy quality, as though this jungle was really one enormous beast. Through a slight gap in the foliage, Jo could see part of some crumbling ruin, eroded and overgrown. Something blobbed on to the screen, accompanied by the now-familiar squelching sound.

Another blob appeared, then another. Jo looked hard. Rain? No, something thicker—and more alive. Jo switched off the scanner and stood thinking. Conditions looked nasty outside. It seemed to be nighttime, and it would probably be cold. She went to a clothing locker in the wall and took out a long-sleeved, hooded coat, and a pair of thick gloves. As she put them on she went back to the Doctor. 'I don't know if you can hear me, Doctor. I'm going to look for help. I'll be back as soon as I can.' With a last look at the still figure on the couch, she slipped the little recorder into her pocket, operated the door-control and went out into the jungle. The door of the TARDIS closed behind her.

Stretched out on the couch, the Doctor was as cold and still as the stone effigy on a Crusader's tombstone.

Outside the TARDIS, the light was murky-green and the air chill. Jo was glad of her warm coat. The TARDIS had landed in the middle of a thicket of spongy, fleshy plants, which seemed to give out a sinister hissing sound. The police box, the TARDIS's exterior form, was covered with blobs of some thick white substance. Even as she watched, one of the spongy plants swayed forward and 'spat' another blob on to the side of the TARDIS. It was as though the arrival of the police box had triggered off some defence mechanism, and the plants were blindly attacking this new enemy. Jo had often heard the Doctor say that the TARDIS was invulnerable to outside attack. Deciding it wasn't likely to be harmed by a few messy plants, she turned to go.

As she moved, something struck her shoulder. One

of the plants had registered her as an enemy and shot a stream of the viscous liquid at her. Shuddering, she wiped it off with her gloved hand. Hurrying out of range of the sponge-plants, Jo pushed her way through the jungle to the ruined structure she had seen on the scanner.

There wasn't much to see when she got there. Crumbling stone pillars, broken walls, a slab of stone that might have been an altar ... Jo guessed she was looking at the ruins of some ancient temple. Proof that there had once been intelligent life on this strange planet, though it could have died out thousands of years ago. On the other hand, reflected Jo, you could probably find just such a ruin in the jungles of Brazil—with a modern super-city only a few miles away. Cheering herself with this reflection, she moved on.

To her great relief, the jungle soon became less dense, giving way to a stretch of sandy ground in which the plants grew more sparsely. She became aware of a change in the quality of the light. The dull green murk was giving way to a yellow glare.

The temperature rose dramatically, and it was dawn, just as if someone had switched on a light. A great yellow sun blazed down from the sky, and Jo found it intolerably hot in the hooded coat. She took it off, noticing with distaste that the splash of fluid from the sponge-plants had turned itself into a thick green mould, which actually seemed to be growing on the coat. She threw it to one side and carried on without it.

Dotted among the other plants were taller reed-like

growths, surmounted with a small round pod, fringed with leaves. In the centre of the pod was an opening, uncannily like the pupil of a human eye. As she passed a clump of these plants, Jo was amused to see the stalks sway towards her, and the eyes of the plants open wide as if in astonishment. But her amusement soon vanished. She heard strange rustlings and weird cries from the thick jungle behind her. Jo hurried on, unable to shake off the uncanny feeling that *something* was following her...

The Doctor's eyes flicked open. He swung his long legs to the ground, stood up and looked round. 'Jo?' he called. 'Jo, where are you?' He listened. All he heard was a continuous slap, slap, slap—as though something was splashing on to the outside of the TARDIS. The Doctor sniffed. Something else was wrong. He went to the console. The instruments showed a breathable atmosphere outside—the TARDIS should have been drawing on *that* for air, first filtering out any undesirable elements. But there was a faintly musty smell in the air. The TARDIS was using its automatic air-supply. For some reason, no air was reaching the TARDIS from outside.

A warning light began to blink on the console. The Doctor looked. A tiny screen was flashing a message. 'AUTOMATIC OXYGEN SUPPLY EX-HAUSTED.'

The Doctor shook his head. He was still feeling muzzy and confused. Everything seemed to be going wrong. 'Just have to use the emergency supply,' he muttered. He touched a control and a wall-panel slid back, revealing three large oxygen cylinders, each surmounted with a glass dial. The Doctor switched on the first one. There was a brief reassuring hiss of oxygen—then silence. The Doctor peered at the little dial—the needle read 'EMPTY'. He tried the second cylinder. The result was the same. The Doctor turned on the third cylinder, and this time the hiss was steady and continuous. He gave a sigh of relief and looked at the dial. The needle wasn't at the EMPTY mark, but it was hovering perilously close. 'Less than an hour's supply,' said the Doctor thoughtfully. He knew he had only himself to blame. It was bad enough letting one back-up system run low, but two...

Registering a mental vow to top up *all* the TARDIS oxygen systems as soon as possible, the Doctor decided that, since air wasn't getting in, he would have to go out. He took a cloak from the wardrobe locker and operated the door control. Nothing happened. The Doctor frowned, re-checked the control circuits, then tried again. Still nothing. He was trapped in the TARDIS.

In the silence the Doctor could hear the steady slap, slap, slap, from outside. The oxygen cylinder hissed away, the needle on its dial flickering steadily closer to the empty mark. When the oxygen was exhausted, he would die...

## 2

## The Invisible Menace

Jo hurried on, making better progress now that the
jungle had thinned out. She noticed something in
front of her and dropped to one knee. In a patch of
soft sand she saw the clear imprint of a foot. A little
further ahead she could see another footprint, and
then another ... She slipped off her glove to feel the
ground, wondering if the footprint was recent or very
old. She crumbled the sand between her fingers, not
noticing how close she had come to the base of one of
the sponge-plants. Suddenly the plant spat milky
liquid at her. Jo jumped back, but a few drops of the
fluid caught the back of her hand. She fished out her
handkerchief and scrubbed the stuff off, throwing
away the handkerchief when she'd finished. Pulling
her glove back on she followed the line of footprints.

They led her through a patch of thicker jungle and
into a clearing. In the centre of the clearing stood the
wreck of a small space-craft, its hull picked out in
blue and gold.

Jo moved cautiously towards it. The ship was small
and stubby, vaguely cigar-shaped. Hull and fins were
badly damaged, and the door hung open. Already a
tracery of jungle vines was growing across the gap.
Which didn't necessarily mean the wreck wasn't a

recent one, thought Jo. Everything probably grew with frightening speed in a jungle like this.

Jo called through the doorway. 'Hello, anybody there?' No reply. Gathering her courage, she climbed inside.

The interior was cramped and gloomy, dimly lit by the greenish light filtering in from the jungle outside. In the nose-cone of the craft, Jo could see a tiny flight-deck. A space-suited figure was sitting in the pilot's seat. Jo moved towards it. The man showed no sign of being aware of her presence. Timidly she tapped him on the shoulder. The swivel chair creaked round, and the body of the spaceship pilot slid gently to the floor, the face behind the helmet-visor stiff and dead.

Jo screamed and backed away ... and a hand came firmly down on her shoulder. Two men stood looking at her. Both were tall and fair-haired, dressed in simple uniforms with a sensible workmanlike look about them. They had wide webbing belts round their waists, from which hung a variety of tools and weapons, and small packs on their backs. The man holding her was very big with a long bony face, at once kindly and stern. The man behind him was smaller, thin-faced and younger, with a fierce angry look about him. In his hand was a blaster, aimed steadily at Jo.

Jo looked fearfully at them. 'Who are you?'

'My name's Taron,' said the big man. 'This is Vaber.'

Vaber holstered his gun. It was clear that he didn't consider her much of a menace. 'Where do you come from?' he demanded. 'What planet?'

'I come from Earth.'

Jo's simple statement brought a surprising reaction. Both men stared incredulously at her. 'There's no such place as Earth,' Vaber said roughly. 'It's just a name in the old legends.'

'How did you get here?' asked Taron.

'In the TARDIS. It's a kind of spaceship.' To Jo's relief they accepted this without question. 'I've a friend with me,' she went on. 'He's desperately ill, he may even be dying. Please, can you help me?'

'Look, we've no time for——' Vaber began speaking roughly, but Taron interrupted him.

'I'm qualified in Space Medicine. I'll do what I can for your friend. Where is this TARDIS?'

'Back through the jungle, close to a sort of ruined temple.'

Taron nodded. 'I think I know the place.'

A third man ran into the spaceship. Like the others he was uniformed and fair-haired. He was very tall and thin, more openly frightened than his two companions. 'Patrol approaching,' he gasped. 'Three or four of them.'

Taron took command. 'All right, Codal, we'll move out.' He turned to Jo. 'You stay here and hide. If we try to take you, you'll only slow us down. We'll lose them in the jungle and come back for you when we can.'

Before Jo could protest all three had fled from the spaceship, leaving her full of unanswered questions. What was this unknown 'Patrol' that caused such alarm?

She went to the door and looked out, but the three

men had already vanished. Jo heard a sudden rustling sound from the patch of dense green jungle at the edge of the clearing. *Something* was forcing its way through it, and it was coming towards her ... Jo ducked back inside the ship and looked quickly round for a hiding place.

She found a tall wardrobe-like wall locker which held spare uniforms and space-suits. Jo slipped inside, huddling behind the rack of garments, and pulled the door closed. There was a slatted ventilation panel in the door, so she could still see outside.

The ship rocked a little and the vines over the door were pushed aside. Jo peered through the panel, and saw—nothing! Yet obviously *someone* had entered the cabin. She could hear hoarse breathing and stealthy, padding footsteps. A plastic beaker rose in the air of its own accord, then dropped to the floor. On the flight deck a pen, a plastic notebook, various navigational instruments rose and fell in the same eerie way. Lockers opened and closed, their contents floating through the air and falling to the ground as the invisible searcher dropped them. The activity was coming nearer. Jo held her locker door tightly closed from the inside. Sure enough, a few minutes later, she felt the unseen something on the other side of the door trying to turn the handle. She clung on desperately. After a moment the pressure stopped and the hoarse breathing moved away.

Jo peeped out. Close to the door, a plastic carton jumped, as though suddenly kicked aside. The little craft tilted, the vines over the door were brushed

17

aside by the unseen form, the craft lurched and then resumed its former position. Jo crept from hiding and went to the door, peering through the curtain of vines. On the marshy ground before the ship a line of footprints was appearing, footprints completely alien in shape. They moved towards the edge of the clearing, the plants rustled and waved, and the invisible intruder was gone.


The Doctor checked all the door-opening circuits and found them in perfect order. Abandoning the control panel console, he tried opening the doors manually. For some time he struggled without success. The doors were held from the outside with a grip that was rubbery yet firm. It yielded, but would not give way.

The hiss of the oxygen cylinder faded and died. A warning light flashed on the centre console. Wearily the Doctor staggered across to it. This time the message on the screen read, 'CABIN ATMOSPHERE SHORTLY UNABLE TO SUSTAIN LIFE.' The Doctor went back to the door and resumed his desperate struggle.

Already he felt consciousness beginning to slip away.


Vaber and Codal crouched in a clump of thick jungle, blasters at the ready. They spun round at the sound of approaching movement. It was Taron. 'I think we've lost them. There were just a few scouts, and they're moving off that way, away from the ship. The girl should be all right. We'd better try to find this friend of hers.'

Vaber looked incredulously at him. 'You don't mean to say you meant it? Why should we waste time on some stranger?'

'Because he's ill. I'm still a doctor, Vaber. Even here.' Taron led the way into the jungle, and the others followed.

When they reached the ruined temple, it took them quite a time to find the TARDIS. They had been looking for some kind of conventional spaceship, until they realised that the tall, oblong shape was the 'Space-Craft' they were seeking. The fact that the TARDIS was coated with the rubbery fungus spat out by the sponge-plants didn't make things any easier.

Taron scratched his head. 'Well, whatever it is, it's the only *new* thing here—so it must be what we want!'

From a belt-pouch he took a tiny square of transparent plastic, which unfolded into a complete protective suit—cape, hood and gauntlets all in one. From his pack he produced a spray which dissolved the rubbery growth covering the TARDIS. When an area was cleared, Taron started to pull the fungus away with his gloved hands. The others joined him, the sponge-spores splashing harmlessly on their protective clothing.

When they'd freed the area around the door, it swung suddenly open, and the Doctor toppled out. They grabbed him and dragged his body clear. The

TARDIS door swung closed behind him, and the sponges resumed their mindless attack.

The Doctor was sucking great whooping breaths into his lungs. As soon as he could speak, he gasped, 'Thank you ... thank you very much indeed. How did you find me?'

Taron briefly told him of meeting Jo in their wrecked space-craft. The Doctor was relieved to hear that, until recently at least, Jo was still all right. Taron turned to Codal. 'Better circle the area, see if there's any more activity.' As Codal slipped away, Taron saw the Doctor staring intently at him. 'Well, what is it?' he said brusquely.

The Doctor said, 'Forgive me. It's just that I seem to know you—all of you! Or rather, I know your people.'

'That's scarcely likely.'

'Oh you never know,' said the Doctor airily. 'I travel quite a bit. Where *are* you from?'

'A planet many systems from here. It's called——'

'Skaro!' said the Doctor triumphantly, answering his own question. 'Of course—you're Thals!'

Taron stared at him. 'How could you possibly know that?'

'I've visited Skaro. I was there at the time of the first Dalek war.'

Taron looked at the tall shape of the TARDIS, now once more obscured by the rubbery spitting of the sponge-plants. 'In our legends, there is a being from another planet, who came to Skaro at our time of greatest peril. He travelled in something called——'

'The TARDIS,' confirmed the Doctor. 'That's it over there.'

'He had three companions,' said Taron slowly.

The Doctor supplied the missing names. 'Barbara, Ian and Susan.'

'Are you trying to tell us that *you* are the Doctor?' demanded Vabor.

'That's right, old chap.'

'That's impossible. The First Dalek War was generations ago, before any of us were born. No one lives that long.'

'Ah, but I'm not a Thal. Besides, don't your legends tell that the TARDIS could also travel through Time?'

Vaber came closer, hand steady on the blaster in his belt. 'And now you turn up here—of all the planets in the galaxy! Well, I don't believe you. You've come to spy on us. Who are you? What are you *really* doing here?'

The Doctor looked calmly at him, trying to make allowances for the fact that Vabor was obviously frightened and exhausted, ready to lash out at any target. 'Now see here, young man,' he said mildly. 'You helped to save my life and I'm grateful, but that doesn't give you the right to interrogate me.'

They were interrupted by Taron. He whipped another aerosol from a belt-pouch and sprayed the Doctor's cheek. The Doctor jumped back. 'What do you think you're doing?'

'There was a splash of that white fluid on your face. It contains the growth-spores of the sponge-plants. The fungus grows very quickly. Without treatment it

21

would have spread all over your body.'

The Doctor shuddered. 'It seems I must thank you for saving my life a second time.'

Jo grew bored waiting for the Thals to return, but she didn't dare venture outside the spaceship. Hunting round the little cabin she found a plastic box of food concentrates, rubbery cubes in several different colours. She ate a couple and found them odd-tasting but satisfying. In a recess she discovered a wash-basin. After a certain amount of fiddling with taps, she managed to produce first drinking-water, and then a stream of warm soapy water in the little basin.

Jo decided on a quick clean-up. It would not only make her feel better, it would help to pass time till the others returned. She pulled off her gloves and started to roll up her sleeves. Then she stopped, gazing in horror at the back of her right hand. A spreading blotch of fungus had grown all over it...

The Doctor listened as his rescuers argued between themselves. It seemed to be a question of whether they should move off at once, or wait for the return of Codal. Eventually it was decided to wait. The Doctor thought he might as well use the time in gathering some information about his new surroundings. 'What's the name of this planet?' he asked.

It was Vaber who answered, speaking with the harsh bitterness that seemed habitual to him. 'Spiridon—one of the nastiest pieces of planetary garbage in this galaxy.'

The Doctor raised his eyebrows. 'Indeed! Is it inhabited?'

'Oh yes! Vegetation with all the nastier characteristics of animal life. Animals that eat everything that moves, including each other. And a climate changing from tropical in the day to freezing at night.'

'Any *intelligent* life-forms?'

'Only the Spiridons. They had a civilisation once, but it's in ruins now.'

'I'd very much like to see one of them.'

Vaber grinned sourly. 'You'll find that difficult. They happen to be invisible.'

There was another important question in the Doctor's mind. He spoke cautiously, feeling his way. 'I gather you're on some kind of special mission here—that you have dangerous enemies?' The Thals looked suspiciously at him, but didn't answer. 'I'm on something of a special mission myself,' continued the Doctor. 'Perhaps we can help each other?'

Taron shook his head. 'I'm sorry, we don't know enough about you to trust you like that.'

'Oh, why don't you tell him?' snarled Vaber. 'We're none of us going to get off Spiridon alive. This is a suicide mission.'

The Doctor looked sharply at him. 'What makes you say that?'

'We *crash*-landed. Our Commander was killed on impact, so Taron here took command. The sub-space radio was wrecked on landing, and the ship's so badly damaged we can never take off again.'

'You *volunteered*, Vaber,' said Taron harshly. 'No one forced you to come.'

For men sharing a desperate mission, they didn't get on very well, thought the Doctor. Quietly he asked. 'How many of you are here?'

'We *were* seven,' said Taron slowly. 'The Commander was killed—and we've lost three more since then.'

'But you still won't accept my help?'

Taron shook his head. 'We'll take you back to your friend, then you're on your own. Our mission is too important to risk on unknowns.'

'You may not trust me yet, Taron, but I have a feeling there's already a very strong link between us. To quote an old Earth proverb—"My enemy's enemy is my friend."'

The lanky Codal suddenly appeared from the jungle. 'Everything's quiet now.'

Taron stood up. 'Let's get moving. Doctor, if you see me signal get under cover fast. And don't make a sound.'

'I *have* been in jungles before,' the Doctor said rather huffily.

'Not like this one,' said Taron grimly.

As they made their way through the jungle, Taron saw that the Doctor could move as silently as any of them. He seemed unaffected by the blazing heat, and showed no signs of tiring as they forced their way through the tough vegetation.

They came to a broad path cutting across the jungle. It had obviously been cleared by some advanced technological means. Touching the severed ends of a vine the Doctor guessed at a wide-beam heat-ray. Taron held up his hand for silence. Something was moving towards them. Curiously enough, they could hear it but not see it. It made a strange clanking, grinding noise, suggesting some complex mechanical device on the point of complete break-down. A blurred trail crept towards them along the charred surface of the path. It wavered and stopped, and the harsh grinding sound died away. Codal looked at Taron. 'What do you think?'

'Sounds like light-wave sickness. That's what the others had.'

'Shall we risk it then? Show our new friend what we're up against?' Vaber had swung into a mood of hysterical cheerfulness. He ran out on to the path, and up to the point where the mysterious tracks ended. He pulled a couple of sprays from his belt pouch, and tossed one to the Doctor. 'Here you are, join in the fun!'

The Doctor looked at the spray. 'Is this some kind of weapon?'

Vaber laughed. 'It's *paint*, that's all. A paint-spray from the ship's stores.'

Vaber touched a nozzle on the top of the little spray, and a mist of bright blue paint shot out. He waved the spray to and fro in front of him, and after a puzzled look at Taron, the Doctor did the same. *His* spray produced a fine mist of gold.

Slowly a shape appeared in the empty air ahead of them. The effect was rather like a 'magic' drawing book where a pencil rubbed across an apparently blank page produces a hidden picture.

This picture, however, was solidly three-dimensional. Standing in the middle of the path, its shape picked out incongruously in blue and gold, was the menacing form of a Dalek.

# 3
## The Deadly Trap

Vaber looked at the Doctor, wondering how he would react. If he expected fear or horror, he was disappointed. The Doctor himself had come to Spiridon in pursuit of the Daleks. Moreover, he had realised from the first that the presence of Thals confirmed that there were Daleks on the planet. Taron's 'special mission' could only be some operation against the hereditary enemies of the Thals. The Doctor started examining the Dalek with an air of brisk competence. He waved a hand in front of the eye-stalk. 'Total loss of vision, motive power nil, weaponry de-activated too—luckily for us!'

Taron was watching him curiously. 'You seem to know a good deal about Daleks.'

'I've had cause. But I've never come across invisible ones before. How do they do it?'

Codal seemed to be the scientist of the party. 'They discovered it by studying the Spiridons. That is the reason they came to this planet. It's some kind of anti-reflecting light wave.' Recognising a fellow spirit, Codal was talking as one dedicated scientist to another. 'Their problem is that to create the energy needed they use enormous amounts of power. They can't sustain it for long. Either they revert to visibility, or they fall victim to light-wave sickness, like this one. Let's take a closer look, shall we?'

Codal was all set to dismantle the Dalek on the spot, but the Doctor held him back. 'Most Daleks have an automatic distress-call. Even when the Dalek is de-activated the transmitter might still go on functioning for a while. We'd better keep moving.'

Some time later Taron halted in a small clearing. 'Codal and I know this area best. We'll scout ahead. Vaber, you stay here with the Doctor.'

Taron and Codal moved away. The Doctor, as always making the best of things, settled himself with his back to a curiously gnarled tree trunk, long legs stretched out before him. 'Your Taron's a cautious fellow.'

'Too cautious,' Vaber muttered protestingly. 'Things'd be different if Miro was still alive.'

The Doctor was examining a clump of oddly shaped plants growing near his tree. 'Miro?'

'Miro was our Commander—he was killed when we landed. Taron is the expedition's doctor. I was Miro's Number Two, but technically Taron outranks me. He took command—and a fine mess he's made of it. He'll go on being cautious till we all get killed.'

The Doctor nodded thoughtfully. Vaber's story accounted for the tensions within the small group of Thals. Taron was a doctor, unaccustomed to active command. Now that the responsibility was his, he might well be ultra-careful, fearful of making some mistake. On the other hand, his attitude might be amply justified. As yet the Doctor knew too little of the situation on Spiridon to form a proper judgement. 'What do *you* think Taron should do?' he asked casually.

Vaber was eager to tell him. 'Attack the Daleks and wipe them out. There are no more than a dozen of them on the planet, just a small scientific party studying invisibility techniques. One determined attack could destroy them all.'

The Doctor nodded thoughtfully. It sounded a very attractive plan. But could things really be that easy? With the Daleks you could never be sure. 'Tell me about the Spiridons,' he said. 'Are they always invisible?'

Vaber abandoned his prowling and sat down at the edge of the clearing. 'Codal says so. According to him, this planet is so hostile they *had* to develop invisibility—he calls it the ultimate in survival techniques.'

Although neither the Doctor nor Codal realised it, the hostility of Spiridon was being demonstrated at this very moment. In the dense jungle behind Vaber, a thick hairy tentacle, about the size of a full-grown python, was stirring. Typically enough for Spiridon, the tentacle belonged not to an animal but to a plant. At the centre of the plant was a fleshy orchid-like growth some twenty feet across. The plant, like many on Spiridon, was carnivorous, and the long tentacles growing out from the centre were designed to capture its prey.

The Doctor was still intent on his clump of plants. He had discovered that if he moved his hand to and fro, an 'eye' opened on the pod, and the plant swayed to and fro as if watching him. 'Fascinating,' he murmured.

Vaber saw what he was doing. 'Useful, too. The plants react whenever one of the invisible Spiridons approaches. We use them as a kind of early warning system.' Unseen, the tentacle slipped closer.

'The Spiridons co-operate with the Daleks, then?' asked the Doctor.

'I don't think they have any choice. The Daleks saturated the jungles with killer rays. Invisibility didn't protect the Spiridons against that kind of thing. The survivors were too terrified to do anything but surrender and co-operate.'

The tentacle was close enough now. It reached out like a whiplash, winding round Vaber's waist and dragging him towards the jungle. Alerted by the screams, the Doctor sprang across the clearing and grabbed Vaber's legs, trying to haul him back. But the tentacle was appallingly strong. The only result was that *both* of them were hauled remorselessly into the jungle. The Doctor heard Vaber gasp. 'Knife ... get knife...'

A heavy jungle knife was sheathed at Vaber's belt. The Doctor grabbed it and hacked savagely at the tentacle. Thick green ichor spurted out. The tentacle unwound from Vaber, lashed about wildly and snaked back into the jungle. Vaber crumpled to the ground, and the Doctor was kneeling over him when Taron rushed in from the other side of the clearing. 'What happened?'

The Doctor waved towards the jungle. 'Something rather nasty was planning on having us for breakfast.'

Vaber struggled to his feet, as if unwilling to show weakness in Taron's presence. 'I'm all right now...' He winced as the effort of speaking sent a stab of pain through his bruised ribs.

Taron looked anxiously at him. 'If you'd like to rest for a while...

'I said I'm all right!' He looked at the Doctor and muttered, 'Thanks.'

The Doctor cleaned the knife in the ground and tossed it back to Vaber. 'Let's call it a useful lesson—on the need for caution at all times! Perhaps Taron is right after all.'

Taron looked puzzled. 'What about?'

The Doctor was looking at Vaber. 'About not rushing headlong into an attack on the Daleks.'

Vaber flared up again. 'If I'm going to die, I want it to be for a better reason than providing nourishment for some flesh-eating plant...'

The quarrel was interrupted by the arrival of Codal. 'What are you all doing? Look at the eye-plants!'

The plants were lashing about in agitation, the fringe of leaves curling closed over the central pod.

'Spiridon patrol,' Taron said curtly. 'We'd better hide.'

He led them into the centre of a clump of low-lying plants, rather like dwarf palm trees. There was space to hide between the thick trunks, and the wide leaves gave good cover. From their vantage-point they could see the jungle all around being thrashed by the movement of unseen presence.

The Doctor studied the pattern of movements.

'The sweep's moving this way. They'll find us if we don't change position soon.'

Vaber reached for his blaster. 'Why don't we attack first? We can ambush them.'

Taron's hand closed on his arm. 'We don't know how many there are! And what do we use as a target if we can't see them?'

Codal said, 'I'll lead them off. You can all get away while they're following me.' Before anyone could stop him, he had left his cover. He started to run through the jungle, making no attempt to conceal himself and generating as much noise as he could.

The othes watched him crash away. Soon there was a quick ripple of movement in the thick green vegetation, a ripple that went off after Codal.

'It's working,' said Taron. 'They're following. Codal's given us our chance. Let's not waste it.'

Wriggling from their hiding-place, they began to run in the opposite direction.

Codal came panting to a halt in the middle of a jungle trail. The Spiridon patrols were a long way behind. With any luck he'd led them far enough to give the others a chance of escape. It was time to begin circling round to re-join them. His thin chest heaving as he gasped for breath, Codal felt astonished at his own audacity. He'd been on the move before he'd realised what had come over him. Maybe he wasn't such a wash-out after all. Codal was the youngest and least experienced of the Thal party, and the question of his own courage was something that pre-occupied him constantly. But his moment of self-congratulation was brief. He saw a clump of eye-plants beside the trail, and realised with a feeling of sudden dread that they were all tightly closed. Suddenly, invisible hands gripped him tightly. He struggled wildly, kicking and punching at his unseen captors, hearing grunts as the wild blows landed. But the struggle was hopeless. The invisible hands tightened their grip, Codal watched helplessly as a chunk of dead wood rose from the side of the trail and flew straight for his head...

Jo Grant was feeling very weak by now. The blotchy fungus had spread half-way up her arm, and seemed to be draining her strength. Her temperature had rocketed, and she was sick and giddy. She felt she ought to keep her 'log' up to date, though there was little enough to say. Fumbling with her left hand, she took the recorder from her pocket and touched the control. 'My hand and arm have become infected by some plant from the jungle. The infection is spreading very rapidly. I don't think the men I met here are coming back, so I'm going to try to get through the jungle and find help.' She switched off the recorder and thrust it clumsily back in her pocket, not noticing that it was only part-way inside. She got to her feet, staggering as a wave of dizziness came over her, and made for the door.

She was attempting to climb down from the space-craft when she heard a thrashing movement in the jungle. The invisible creature was returning! Terrified, Jo turned and went back inside, intending to return to her hiding-place in the locker. She didn't realise that the recorder had dropped to the ground outside the ship. The effort of moving was too much for her. The cabin spun round and everything went black.

The jungle rustled as the Spiridon forced its way through the vegetation. It paused at the edge of the clearing, moved across to the little space-craft and climbed aboard. Jo's body was sprawled in plain sight in the centre of the cabin. The Spiridon moved curiously towards her...

Safe in a new hiding-place, Taron, Vaber and the Doctor waited as long as they dared for Codal to reappear. Finally Taron stood up. 'We'd better make for the spaceship. Maybe he'll rendezvous with us there.'

'Or maybe we're down to two, now.' Vaber spoke sourly. Taron said nothing. He led the way through the jungle, and the Doctor followed, Vaber trailing sulkily behind. It took them a long time to reach the spaceship. Taron moved with his usual caution, insisting on a wide detour to avoid further patrols.

But at last they came to the edge of the clearing. The wrecked spaceship was still sitting in the middle of it. The Doctor pressed forward, eager to be reunited with Jo, but Taron held him back. 'Wait— there's movement on the other side of the clearing.' To the Doctor's horror, four Daleks glided out of the jungle, grouping themselves in a semi-circle around the little ship. The Doctor heard the familiar, hated voice cutting through the jungle air.

'Dalek patrol calling Command Centre. Thal space-craft has been located. We shall destroy according to instructions.' The Daleks widened their semi-circle. The patrol leader ordered, 'Prepare to fire.'

The Doctor started to get up. Taron tried to stop him. 'There's nothing you can do.'

The Doctor threw off his grip. 'Jo's inside there! I've *got* to stop them.'

The Dalek voice ordered, 'Fire!' Before the order could be carried out, the Doctor ran forward, placing himself between the ship and the Dalek guns. 'Wait! You mustn't shoot, there's someone inside.'

For a moment the Daleks froze, as if stunned by the audacity of the interruption. Then the patrol leader spoke. 'Disable prisoner. Save for interrogation.' Instantly a Dalek fired and the Doctor's feet were smashed from under him by an agonising blast of pain. As he crashed to the ground he heard the Dalek voice again. 'Proceed as ordered. Fire!'

His legs numb and useless, the Doctor called, 'No, you mustn't...'

Above his head the Dalek guns blazed in unison. The little spaceship glowed cherry red and exploded in a blast of flame.

# 4
# In the Power of the Daleks

Unable to bear the sight of the blazing space-craft, the Doctor lowered his eyes to the ground. A few feet away he saw a familiar black shape—the TARDIS log-recorder. Automatically he reached out for it and thrust it in his pocket. A Dalek loomed over him. 'Stand up.'

The Doctor tried. Agonising pins-and-needles shot through his legs, and he stumbled and fell.

'Stand up or we will exterminate you now.'

Painfully the Doctor got to his feet. The Dalek herded him forward. 'Walk!'

The Doctor stumbled slowly away between his captors. At the edge of the clearing he stopped to look back at the still-blazing ship. 'Move.' The Daleks ordered him forward. As the Dalek patrol and its prisoner disappeared into the jungle, Taron and Vaber came out of hiding.

Vaber looked after the departing Daleks. 'We should have helped him.'

Taron shook his head, gazing into the flames. 'There was nothing we could do ... nothing.'

Feeling gradually came back to the Doctor's legs during the long march through the jungle, but he was glad when their destination came in sight. It was nothing more than a small, squat blockhouse. The door slid open to reveal a lift, and the patrol passed inside.

The Doctor was quite unsurprised by this development. It was normal Dalek practice to install their bases underground whenever possible. Daylight and open air meant nothing to them, and they flourished best in a controlled underground environment.

The lift plunged down and down, and the Doctor cupped his hands over his ears as they popped under the changing pressure. At last the lift shuddered to a halt and they all filed out. They were in a long straight corridor, apparently cut from solid rock. At intervals in either direction other corridors intersected across their one.

The Doctor was taken to a heavy metal door. A Dalek touched a control, the door opened and the Doctor was thrust inside. The door closed behind him.

It was no surprise to the Doctor to find himself in a bare, metal cell. What did surprise him was to see Codal crouched in one corner, his head in his hands. The young scientist looked up in astonishment. 'Doctor!' Then his face fell. 'So it was all for nothing. They got you after all.'

'Not all of us. Taron and Vaber are still free.'

Briefly the Doctor explained how he'd been captured. Codal told the Doctor of his own capture. 'I don't understand why they didn't kill me,' he concluded.

'I'm afraid they're saving us both for interrogation,' said the Doctor. 'They'll want to know what we're doing on this planet.'

Codal shuddered, terrified at the thought of Dalek questioning. The Doctor could see he needed cheering up. 'I haven't thanked you for giving us that chance to escape. It was very brave of you.'

Codal laughed bitterly. 'Brave? Me? I've been in terror since we landed on this planet.'

The Doctor nodded. 'That's natural enough. We're all afraid at times.'

'Taron and Vaber know how to deal with fear. I'm a scientist, not a soldier. I'm not used to danger.'

'I thought all your force were volunteers?'

'We were!' said Codal gloomily. 'I was the only scientist young and fit enough to come on the expedition. Everyone expected me to volunteer, so I did. I didn't even have the courage to be the odd man out.'

The Doctor chuckled. 'Courage isn't a matter of not feeling frightened, you know.'

'Then what is it?'

'It's being afraid, but doing what you have to do anyway. Just as you did. You're a very brave man, Codal.'

Codal smiled wryly. 'I'm not convinced. But thanks anyway. Well, what do we do now?'

'We start trying to find a way out of here. Now let's see if we've got anything useful. Did they search you?'

'No, not really. Just took away my blaster and my knife.'

'Then turn out your pockets. You never know.' The Doctor began searching his own pockets, but the first thing he found made him pause in sorrow. It was the log-recorder Jo had taken from the TARDIS. He switched it on playback, listening to Jo's voice. 'The

Doctor appears to have fallen into a deep coma...'
He played the tape through, learning of Jo's leaving
the TARDIS, her meeting with the Thals. He shuddered at the description of her infection by the
fungus. Perhaps her end had been a merciful one
after all.


Jo Grant awoke from a nightmare-haunted sleep to
find herself lying on a pile of skins in a tiny cave. She
could see a greenish glow of jungle light coming from
the vine-covered entrance. She became aware that her
temperature had gone down, and the throbbing in
her arm had almost vanished. She looked at her hand
and arm. They were covered with a thick yellowish
paste, and beneath it the stain of the fungus had re-
ceded.

Jo blinked and looked round the cave. A wooden
bowl was hovering in the air, and a bunch of brightly
coloured berries was squeezing itself into it. One of
the invisible creatures from the spaceship was in the
cave with her. Jo kept perfectly still. The bowl floated
towards her. She heard the sound of hoarse breathing,
and then a whispering voice. 'Do not be afraid. I want
only to help you.'

Since there was no one else to talk to, Jo spoke to
the wooden bowl. 'Who are you?'

'My name is Wester. I am a Spiridon. Drink this
juice. It will help you to cast off the effect of the
fungoid infection.'

The bowl bobbed nearer. Jo took it and drank the
juice, which seemed tart and sweet at the same time.

She felt a glow through her body.

'The infection is almost gone,' whispered the ghostly voice. 'This will clear it completely.'

Jo drained the bowl and an unseen hand took it and put it to one side. 'What's happened?' she asked confusedly. 'Where are we?'

'We are in a cave near the Dalek City. I found you unconscious in a space-craft and brought you here. Soon after, the Daleks destroyed the ship.'

'*Why* did you help me?' asked Jo. A wave of dizziness came over her. 'There's so much I want to ask you,' she said faintly. 'I don't know where to start.'

'You must rest while the juice takes its full effect,' said the Spiridon voice. 'Afterwards we shall talk...'

Jo nodded, sleepily, letting herself drift away.

When she awoke some time later, she was fresh and alert. To her delight, all traces of the infection were gone from her hand and arm. Wester fed her on strange-looking fruits, and as she ate he told her of the sad state to which the Daleks had reduced his planet. 'They bombarded our world with bacteria and deadly rays. Spiridon became a planet of the Daleks. Only a handful of my people survived, and they were forced to co-operate with the Daleks in their attempt to discover the secret of invisibility.'

'But *you* don't co-operate?'

'A few of us do what we can to resist them ... it's little enough. I hoped the aliens might help us, but they are being killed one by one. Another was captured today—though he looked different from the others.'

Jo's interest was aroused. 'What did he look like?'

'Tall with white hair. His clothes were different.'

'The Doctor!' said Jo excitedly. 'He must have recovered after I left the TARDIS. Trust him to get straight into trouble. I've got to help him.'

'That is not possible,' whispered the Spiridon sadly. 'The Daleks will interrogate him, then use him in their light-wave experiments. He would be better dead.'


The Doctor put away his sonic screwdriver with an angry frown. 'Hopeless. If there's one thing the Daleks are good at, it's making locks!'

Codal shook his head sadly. 'Well, if we can't get the door open...'

The Doctor took up the thought. 'Then we must make our escape when the door is *already* open.'

'By which time there'll be at least one Dalek standing there.' Codal spoke with gloomy relish.

The Doctor was not discouraged. 'Exactly. We've been looking at the problem in the wrong way. We're not trying to deal with a *door*—we're trying to deal with a *Dalek!*'

'How?' asked Codal simply.

The Doctor rubbed his chin. 'I'm not sure yet.' He poked irritably at the pile of objects they'd unearthed from their pockets. 'There must be *something* useful here ...' He picked up the little recorder. 'A small but very efficient electric motor—with a built-in atomic power source ... now if I dismantle the circuitry, reverse the polarity and convert it to a receiver–transmitter with positive feedback ...'

41

He looked expectantly at Codal who said, 'I see! The Dalek guidance system functions by means of high frequency radio-impulses...'

'...And if I can jam those impulses—the Dalek should develop a nice little brain-storm.' Eagerly the Doctor set to work.

In the central control area, the Dalek Commander, military leader of the expedition to Spiridon, was listening to the report of his second-in-command. 'Scientific section request that after interrogation, prisoners should be transferred to their laboratory for light-wave experiments.' The Commander looked across at the laboratory, a sealed-off section separated from the control area by a glass wall.

'Agreed. What of the rest of the Thal expedition?'

'Two Thals estimated still at liberty. Their capture is inevitable.'

In a secluded jungle clearing, Vaber and Taron were digging furiously. As he worked, Vaber thought grudgingly that for once Taron's obsessive caution had paid off. As soon as they had crash-landed, Taron had decided that the Daleks were certain to discover the spaceship sooner or later. Almost his first action had been to order the transport of their precious explosives to this hidden cache in the jungle.

Taron grunted as his fingers touched plastic wrapping. After a little more digging he lifted out a large bundle and set it on the ground.

Exultantly Vaber helped him to unwrap it, and looked in satisfaction at the stubby cylindrical bombs with their attached timing and detonating devices. 'There's enough explosive here to wipe out fifty Daleks. We can rush the blockhouse, blow the lift-shaft and bury the lot of them for ever.'

'Suppose we don't make it to the lift-shaft? I won't take unjustified risks, Vaber. There are only two of us now, and you know what it means if we fail. We'll move when we have a plan that I think has a chance of succeeding, and not before.'

Vaber looked on appalled as Taron started to re-wrap the explosives. He drew his blaster. 'Hand over those bombs.'

Taron glanced up, saw the blaster and went on working. 'No.'

'Give them to me. I'll kill you if I have to.'

Taron finished wrapping the bundle and started to bury it. 'Then you'll have to kill me.'

Vaber glared helplessly at him, unnerved by Taron's calm. There was a sudden roar, a blast of heat, and something shot over their heads to vanish behind a near-by hill. Vaber looked after it. 'That was a space-craft,' he said. 'Coming in to land too low and too fast. Come on!'

He ran towards the little hill. Taron, cautious as ever, finished burying the explosives then ran after him.

It didn't take long to find the wrecked space-craft—the plume of black smoke soaring above the jungle made an excellent guide. They were almost in sight of it when there came a dull roar, and a blast of heat that knocked them off their feet. 'It's blown up,' said Taron, as they picked themselves up.

'Let's hope they got out in time.'

They heard someone pushing through the jungle towards them and waited. A tall, fair-haired girl in Thal Space Uniform staggered out of the jungle, her face blackened with smoke.

Taron recognised her at once, and ran to her. 'Rebec! What happened?'

The girl looked at him dazedly. 'Our glide angle was too steep. We overheated coming through the atmosphere. The ship blew just after we landed.'

'Any other survivors?'

'Marat and Latep ... just behind me.'

Vaber came forward. 'Why did you come? How did you know we needed help?'

The girl shook her head as if to clear it. 'When you didn't report by sub-space radio, we guessed you must be in trouble. Then Communications intercepted another Dalek space signal. This time they managed to crack the code. Once we'd read it, we had to warn you ...'

'Warn us? What about?'

'About the Dalek force on Spiridon.'

'We know that already,' said Vaber impatiently. 'There are only about a dozen of them.'

Rebec shook her head. 'That's what we thought when we sent you. But we were wrong. The signal we intercepted was to Dalek Supreme Command. It said the Dalek force on Spiridon was now complete. Somewhere on this planet are ten thousand Daleks!'

# 5
## The Escape

Even Vaber had to admire the stolid calm with which Taron took this shattering news. He nodded and said, 'This means we must act immediately.' He turned to Rebec. 'Are you fit enough to move? The Daleks will send a patrol very soon to investigate the crash.'

Rebec said, 'I'm all right—just a bit shaken.'

Two more Thals came out of the jungle, one a tall muscular man with a fresh open face, the other scarcely more than a boy. Taron greeted them calmly. 'Marat, Latep, are you all right? We can talk later. Right now it's important to get out of the area.'

With a cheeky grin, young Latep answered for both of them. 'We're fine. Came down with a bit of a bang, that's all. Marat always was a terrible pilot.'

Marat grinned, aiming a playful mock-punch at his smaller friend. 'No one else would have got you here at all!'

Taron spoke seriously. 'It's good to see you—all of you. We'd better be moving.'

The small group of Thals disappeared into the jungle.

Just outside the city, Jo Grant crouched in hiding, Wester beside her. Not that Wester needed to hide, she thought, since he was invisible anyway. By now Jo was quite accustomed to the unseen presence of the Spiridon, and to the ghostly whispering in her ear. She parted the leaves and peered through the gap. She could see the blockhouse, Dalek guards patrolling all round it. Figures in furs and skins were carrying great basket-loads of vegetation through the blockhouse doors. 'Who are they?' she asked.

'They are Spiridons, enslaved by the Daleks.'

'But I can *see* them.'

'You see the robes they wear. The Daleks have ordered our people to wear such robes. They must be visible at all times.'

'What's that stuff they're taking into the city?'

'Samples of our vegetation. The Daleks are experimenting with plant-destroying bacteria.'

Jo looked at the baskets. They were really enormous wire crates. It took two of the Spiridon slaves to carry one. 'If I could get into one of those baskets, I'd be carried straight past the Dalek guards.'

'It is too dangerous,' hissed Wester.

Jo ignored him. 'Whereabouts would they be likely to take the Doctor?'

'Prisoners are always held on the lower levels. He is probably on level seven.'

'I'm going to try it,' said Jo. 'Come on, let's work our way round to that patch of jungle.'

Getting into one of the baskets proved surprisingly easy. They made their way to the edge of the jungle and crept up on a party of Spiridon slaves working under the supervision of a Dalek guard. Jo edged as near to the baskets as she dared, while Wester moved

46

noisily about in the jungle on the other side of the clearing. The Dalek guard registered the noise and moved to investigate. The slaves watched the guard, chattering excitedly together in their hissing voices. Jo slipped unobserved into a nearly-full basket, burying herself under the thick vegetation. The Dalek guard, finding nothing, herded the Spiridon slaves back to work. Soon two of them picked up her basket and started carrying it towards the city.

Jo lay under the vegetation, her heart pounding. She hoped that getting *out* of the Dalek city would prove as easy as getting in.

Taron and the other Thals stood shivering in the middle of a strange, icy landscape. They had climbed a range of low, rocky hills covered with a thick coating of icy slush. They were dotted with gaping, cavernous openings rather like giant pot-holes, and it was to the edge of one of these sinister apertures that Taron had led them. The edge of the hole was rimmed with ice and snow.

Rebec crumbled a piece of the ice between her fingers. 'There's something odd about this stuff—it's well below freezing point, but it's still *soft*...'

Taron nodded. 'Codal called it an allotrope—ice in a different form from the kind we know. He says the core of this planet is a solid mass of the stuff. Every so often, the pressure builds up and the ice pours out of these holes.'

Marat peered into the hole. 'Sort of a cold volcano?'

'That's right. Codal calls it an "icecano".'

'Very interesting, Taron,' said Marat. 'Now tell us why you brought us here—and why you sent Vaber and Latep back for the explosives?'

'When we first landed on this planet, I ordered a full reconnaissance of the area around the Dalek city. I formed a plan to destroy it. But things went wrong. First we lost three men in an ambush, then Codal was captured. That left myself and Vaber. My plan wouldn't work with just two men so I abandoned it, started looking for another. Now you're here we can revert to the original idea.' Taron drew a long breath after what, for him, had been a very long speech. He went on, 'When the Daleks built their underground city, they used this icecano to provide a cooling system. Apparently they needed very low temperatures for their experiments.'

'I wonder why,' Rebec said thoughtfully. 'Invisibility is a problem of light-waves, temperature's got nothing to do with it.'

Taron ignored the interruption. 'The Daleks drove shafts out to meet the natural fissures. If we go down one of these outlets and work our way along to the junctions, we could reach the heart of their city unseen, plant charges at strategic spots and blow the whole place up.'

Rebec looked into the dark icy hole and shivered. 'And suppose this icecano thing erupts while we're down there?'

Taron said nothing. The answer was obvious enough.

Maret was looking down the icy slope. 'Vaber and Latep are coming,' he called.

Slipping and sliding on the icy rock, the two Thals toiled up to rejoin their friends. Vaber was carrying a plastic bundle. He unwrapped the bombs and shared them out. The Thals stowed them away in their back-packs. Vaber looked alert and eager, his normal sulkiness transformed by the prospect of action. 'I've changed the hiding-place of the rest of the explosives, as you ordered, Taron,' he said. 'I've marked the position on this map.' He showed Taron a crumpled piece of paper. 'X marks the spot!'

Taron took the paper and studied it. 'I know the place. Here, Marat, you take this—just in case.' He turned to the others. 'We'd better get started. The fact that there's an army of Daleks in that city makes its destruction a matter of top priority. Vaber, you and Latep take your bombs and find another opening, closer to the main entrance of the city. Blow up the main lift-shaft and the whole place will be buried. The rest of us will attack from this end.'

Taron produced a coil of fine plastic rope from his pack and slung it over his shoulder. He touched a control in his belt. 'Switch on your heating units, all of you, it's going to be cold down there.' Poised on the edge of the hole, Taron looked round the little group, his eyes lingering on Rebec for a moment. He swung a leg over the edge, and Vaber went to help him. 'Taron,' he whispered, 'I'm sorry—about what happened.'

'Forget it.' Taron scrambled over the edge and slid down into the darkness. Vaber and Latep helped Rebec and Marat to follow him down. Then they turned and ran, looking for the hole that would provide their own entrance to the Dalek city.

The Doctor finished his work on the reassembled recorder, fitting the parts tidily back into the box. He looked up at Codal. 'Well, that's the best I can do. Only one thing we need now—a Dalek to try it on!'

Codal said nervously, 'I think you're going to get your wish. I can hear the lift.'

A few minutes later the door opened and a Dalek entered the cell. Codal and the Doctor were sitting innocently in the corner. The Doctor's hands were behind him.

'Prisoners will stand,' ordered the Dalek. Slowly they got up. 'You will be taken for interrogation. Move!'

The Dalek stood waiting just inside the door. The Doctor and Codal moved forward. When they were close enough, the Doctor shouted, 'Now!'

Codal leaped on the Dalek, jamming it against the wall. His shoulder to the metal casing, he grabbed the Dalek's gun-stick, forcing it upwards. At the same time the Doctor jumped behind the Dalek and pressed the re-built recorder to its headpiece.

The Dalek struggled violently in Codal's grip. It was amazingly strong and he knew he couldn't hold it for long. 'Surrender immediately, or you will be exterminated,' grated the harsh voice. Then almost immediately it changed its sound. The pitch became higher and there was a note of hysteria. 'Surrender, surrender ... I am losing control, I am losing control . . .' Suddenly the words garbled together in an agonised electronic shriek. Wrenching free of Codal's grip, the Dalek began hurling itself about the cell, crashing and rebounding from one wall to another like a bee trapped in a bottle. Codal and the Doctor jumped desperately about in the confined space, trying to avoid being crushed. The recorder was knocked from the Doctor's hand. At last the Dalek zoomed straight at the wall, crashed into it, rebounded, spun round and was still.

Gasping, Codal looked at the Doctor. 'That's a very effective little machine.'

'Not any more,' said the Doctor sadly. He picked the crushed recorder from the floor. In the confusion it had been stepped on by the Doctor and run over by the Dalek. It tinkled when the Doctor shook it, 'Still it's served its purpose.' He glanced at the inert Dalek. 'Much as I abhor violence, I rather enjoyed that.' He went to the still-open door. 'Come on, Codal. We can get out of this cell now—but we're a long way from being free.'


The basket was put down with a thump, and Jo peered cautiously out. She was in a long, wide corridor. Fur-clad Spiridon slaves were emptying the baskets into metal bins and pushing them into what seemed to be a huge laboratory. Others were carrying the empty baskets away. Clearly, it wouldn't do for Jo to be still in her basket when it was tipped out. She slipped out of the crate, keeping the stack between her and the Spiridons, and ran off.

51

She obviously couldn't stay in the open—Daleks or Spiridons were bound to spot her. Jo decided to look for a hiding-place while she thought out her next move, and crept cautiously through the next door in the corridor.

It took her into a huge rock-walled area, packed with various kinds of Dalek scientific equipment. Jo guessed it was their control centre. Behind a glass wall dividing the area, they were moving about on various mysterious tasks. There were more Daleks in the control area but they were all some distance away with their backs to her.

Jo looked round for a hiding-place. Like most of the Dalek underground city, the room seemed to have been carved from solid rock, and the walls weren't quite regular in shape. Huge gleaming instrument consoles had been lined up against the rock walls but they weren't completely flush with it. There was a gap, rather like that between a sofa and a wall, into which a very small person might squeeze. Thankful, not for the first time for her lack of size, Jo slipped behind the nearest console and worked her way along the gap until she was completely concealed.

Suddenly, a dial close to her hiding-place began to give out a sharp pinging sound. Two of the Daleks moved across to it, and Jo could hear their voices on the other side of the bank of instruments. 'Sensors detect ice eruption imminent.'

'Prepare to close all cooling ducts. Activate closure when warning dial reaches red alert.'

'I obey.'

One of the Daleks returned to its place on the far side of the room. But the other stayed where it was, evidently watching the warning dial. In its present position it would certainly see Jo if she tried to get away. Her hiding-place had become a trap.

The news of the ice eruption, meaningless to Jo, was a deadly threat to Taron and his party. They were working their way along the ice fissure, which by now had broadened out into a sizeable tunnel, hoping it would lead them to the Dalek city. An icy wind sprang up, accompanied by a low rumbling noise. They struggled forward against it as long as they could, until they came to a point where the tunnel branched. They stopped and the Thals looked at Taron in inquiry. The noise of the wind was too great to allow talking but Taron made a gesture that they should wait. He ran a little way down the right-hand tunnel, then stopped in horror. A wall of ice completely blocked the tunnel—and it was moving towards him.

Taron turned and ran back to the fork, making signs to his little group that they should turn down the left-hand path. Rebec shook her head, pointing back the way they had come, obviously suggesting that they should give up and go back. But even as she pointed, the wall of the fissure cracked open and more ice flooded through, blocking their retreat. There was only one way they could go. As they ran down the left-hand fork the ice appeared behind them, pursuing them down the tunnel.

The Doctor and Codal had almost succeeded in reaching the lift when a Dalek appeared round a corner. Luckily it was as surprised as they were. They turned and ran, disappearing round a corner as the Dalek fired. The Dalek's lights flashed agitatedly and it began screeching, 'Alert! Alert! Alert!'

The message was received in the central control room where Jo crouched in hiding. Again she heard Dalek voices.

'Level seven reports prisoners are at liberty.'

'Instigate condition of maximum alert. Normal operations will cease until prisoners are recaptured.'

'I obey.'

A moment's pause and then another voice, speaking over a public-address system. 'All Daleks will report to lower levels. Maximum security search to commence immediately. Locate and destroy prisoners. Locate and destroy!'

In her hiding place, Jo Grant listened excitedly to the Dalek voices. She was sure the Doctor was one of the escaped prisoners. Trust him to get away without her help. Jo desperately wanted to make her way to the lower levels to find him, but she couldn't—not while the Dalek maintained its stand. Ironically, positions had reversed. Somewhere in the Dalek city the Doctor was free—but Jo herself had become the Daleks' prisoner.

# 6

## Danger on Level Zero

Codal and the Doctor pelted frantically along the complex of corridors, dodging round corner after corner as more and more Daleks appeared. The Doctor, however, was not running completely at random. He led them round three sides of a square back to the lift for which they had originally been heading. At last the lift door came in sight, the doors standing invitingly open. The Doctor and Codal hurled themselves inside—and a Dalek appeared in the lift corridor.

The Doctor stabbed frantically at the lift controls. It took the astonished Dalek a moment to register their presence. By the time it had raised its gun-stick to fire the lift doors were already sliding closed. They came together just as the Dalek fired, the blast of its gun scorching the metal doors.

Inside the lift the Doctor was stabbing at the 'UP' control. Nothing happened. 'They must have operated the master control,' he said. 'Well, what won't go up, must go down.' He touched the 'DOWN' control, and the lift began its smooth descent.

The Doctor let it take them down a few stages, stopped the lift and opened the doors. They slid back to reveal a waiting Dalek. It had time to fire only once before the Doctor closed the doors and sent the lift on its way. Codal looked at the scorch-mark on the back wall of the lift. 'They want to force us down to the lower levels, Doctor. They'll be waiting for us!'

The Doctor rubbed his chin. 'Well if we've got to go down to the basement, we must try and get there before them.' He ripped off the panel by the controls, made a few adjustments with his sonic screwdriver. 'Hold tight, Codal, we're dropping to level zero—non-stop!'

He touched a control, there was a shower of sparks, and the lift dropped like a stone. Codal sank to the floor, hands over his ears, which were popping with the rapidly changing pressure.

The lift stopped with a jarring thump, and the Doctor opened the door. They saw a gloomy, dimly-lit area with rock-walled corridors stretching off in several directions. The whole place looked primitive and functional, less finished than the higher levels. The Doctor guessed that this would be where the basic maintenance machinery of the Dalek city was kept. He led the way along a corridor, more or less at random. The first priority was to find a safe hiding-place. After that they'd just have to take things as they came.

He had chosen a corridor that seemed dark and deserted, hoping that it would lead well away from the main centres of activity. Although the Doctor didn't realise it, the corridor ran along the outer edge of the city. It was empty because it had been evacuated. It was part of the area most endangered by icecano eruptions. Along the corridor at regular intervals were metal grilles flanked with heavy metal shutters. At the moment the shutters were drawn back, and an icy blast of cold air streamed through each grille. The Doctor shivered, wondering why the Daleks needed to keep this area so cold. As they passed yet another of the grilles, he heard a grinding, rumbling sound. It seemed to be getting closer.

The sound was very close indeed for Taron, Rebec and Marat. They were crawling along a rapidly narrowing ice fissure, with the wall of ice rumbling steadily in pursuit. It was hard to move quickly in the confined and slippery space, and Taron had a terrible feeling that the ice was gaining on them. Above the steady rumbling of the moving ice he heard Rebec shout, 'Look, up ahead. It's the shaft...'

Ahead on the left, a square-cut shaft, obviously Dalek-made, led off from the natural fissure at right angles. They reached it just in time. The ice wall surged forward with unexpected speed, and it was almost on their heels when they entered the shaft.

They were in a small square tunnel, fairly short, which ended in a heavy metal grille. Taron peered through. On the other side was a dimly lit, rock-walled corridor—and someone was coming along it. Taron peered through the grille in astonishment as two figures approached. 'Doctor! Codal,' he called.

The Doctor was equally astonished to hear the voice of Taron floating out of the air. He ran to the grille and was just able to make out Taron crouching on the other side. 'I don't suppose this is the moment to ask how you got in there,' he said mildly. 'All the same, I'd be fascinated to know...'

'Doctor, help me free the grille,' interrupted Taron. 'We're trapped in this shaft and the ice is moving up behind us.'

(In the Dalek control room on the upper levels, the Dalek watching the ice monitor saw the dial creep into the danger area. From her hiding place Jo heard it say,

'Ice eruption endangering perimeter corridors. Cooling duct shutters now being closed down.' The Dalek touched a control.)

With the Doctor and Codal tugging on one side, and Taron and Marat pushing from the other, the metal grille didn't stand a chance. It gave way with a shriek of rending metal. The Doctor threw it to one side—just as the heavy, electrically-operated shutters started to close.

The Doctor and Codal acted together, each seizing the edge of the shutter and struggling to hold it back. Taron wedged himself longways between the closing shutters, shoulders against one, boots against the other.

The cooling shaft was almost filled with ice now, and Marat could feel its clammy bulk pressing against him. 'Hurry,' he yelled. 'It's going to crush us!'

Despite the effort of all three men, Taron's powerful body was slowly being folded in two by the pressure of the twin shutters. Quickly Rebec clambered over him. Marat followed. Codal and the Doctor gave a final heave, the Doctor shouted, 'Now Taron!' and Taron rolled out into the corridor. Thankfully the Doctor and Codal let go, and the shutters slammed closed, a thin trickle of ice trapped between their edges.

The Doctor helped Taron to his feet. There was a babble of greetings and explanations. Suddenly Codal yelled, 'Daleks! Run, everybody!'

Two Daleks had appeared in the corridor. The Doctor led his party at a run in the other direction, dodging and weaving to escape the blast of Dalek guns.

The two Daleks followed in pursuit. As they reached the shaft through which Taron and the others had escaped, the metal shutters buckled inwards. A gushing flood of ice poured into the corridor, burying the Daleks.

The Doctor paused, looking back over his shoulder. 'Now there's a bit of luck,' he said cheerfully. 'Let's get away from here.'

Once again, news of the Doctor's progress was relayed to the Dalek control room. 'Prisoners have been driven to level zero. All ascent areas sealed off. All units proceed to level zero immediately.' Daleks began gliding from the room, but the one near Jo remained in his place. She was still trapped.

The Doctor and his friends got quite some way before they ran into the next Dalek patrol. The corridor behind them was sealed off by the ice, but Daleks had meanwhile been pouring in from the upper levels, and it was inevitable that the fugitives would eventually be discovered. They turned a corner to find half-a-dozen Daleks waiting in ambush.

Spinning round they ran desperately down the nearest side corridor, dodged down another, and found themselves trapped. This corridor ended in a pair of massive metal doors. Another, smaller door, also closed, stood just to the left of them.

The Doctor looked at the control panel beside the doors. 'Both locked,' he said. 'This is some kind of security area.' Working with amazing speed he un-screwed the control panel, and began using his sonic screwdriver. 'If I can over-ride the security seal...' With agonising slowness the larger doors started to slide apart. The gap widened until it was almost big enough to admit a body.

Daleks appeared at the far end of the corridor. Their harsh voices rang out. 'Surrender immediately or you will be exterminated!'

Marat, at the rear of the little group, glanced nervously at the slowly opening doors, then at the advancing Daleks. Five people had to get through those doors, *and* close them again, before the Daleks were near enough to fire. There wasn't enough time. Before anyone could stop him, Marat yelled, 'Get inside, all of you!' Drawing his blaster he began running towards the Daleks.

As if astonished, the Daleks halted their advance. Marat had time to fire only once. A Dalek spun round under the effect of his blaster and immediately the rest of the Daleks fired in unison. Marat's smoking body was slammed across the corridor.

By now Rebec, Codal and Taron were through the gap. The Doctor sent an anguished look after Marat, realised he was beyond help and went through the doors himself. On the other side he worked quickly on the controls and the heavy doors began sliding closed again. The edges touched just as the first Daleks reached them and opened fire. The Doctor made a few more adjustments, and leaped back as there was a shower of sparks and a bang. 'Fused solid,' he said with satisfaction. 'They won't open them with the controls, that's for sure.'

Rebec was sobbing in Taron's arms. He patted her awkwardly on the back. 'There's nothing we can do for him now,' he said gruffly.

The Doctor came over to them. 'Oh yes there is! Marat sacrificed himself to buy us a little more time. We owe it to him to make good use of it.' Rebec nodded, stifling her sobs. The Doctor looked round. 'Now what sort of a place is this, I wonder?'

They were in a huge, circular, rock-walled chamber, with a domed roof. Massive Dalek machines hummed and throbbed around them. The Doctor crossed to examine them, looking at the rows of dials and switches. 'It's some kind of refrigeration unit,' he said. 'This must be the cooling chamber. Now, with all that ice around, why do the Daleks need to make it colder still? You could freeze an ocean with a unit this size.'

'Well, at least we're safe for a while,' said Rebec shakily. 'There's no other door, and if that one's really sealed...'

'Don't underestimate the Daleks,' warned the Doctor. 'They won't let a little thing like a solid metal door deter them for long.'

Codal was examining the far side of the room, where a big metal cowl like a chimney-piece projected out from one wall. 'Look at this,' he called. They crossed to join him. He was standing directly under the cowl, pointing upwards. A huge circular 'chimney' with gleaming metal walls stretched up above them. It went up and up until it ended in a tiny dot of blue, almost out of sight.

'Some kind of ventilation shaft,' said the Doctor. 'Seems to go clear up to the surface!'

Taron grunted. 'No use to us. Too wide and too smooth to climb.'

The Doctor nodded absently, the tiny spark of an idea glowing somewhere in his mind. He ducked out from under the cowling, and wandered across the room. Some of the machinery in one corner was evidently under repair. It was covered with huge protective sheets of transparent plastic. The Doctor tested it between his fingers. It was fine, but seemed very strong. He looked at the coils of plastic rope slung over the shoulders of the Thals. The Doctor ran his fingers through his hair, his mind full of calculations about weight, lift and gravity. A scream from Rebec interrupted him. 'Doctor, look at the door!'

A tiny glowing, smoking point had appeared in the metal of the door. As they watched the point started to move downwards, forming the beginnings of a line...

'They're cutting through the door,' said Taron.

The Doctor shot him a look. 'Well, it was pretty obvious they'd do something of that sort. You've got to admire their technology, haven't you?'

Taron looked at him as if he were mad. 'Doctor, it's only a matter of time before they're in here. What are we going to do?'

The Doctor's voice was almost apologetic. 'Well, as a matter of fact I do have an idea. But I'm afraid it's rather bizarre...'

Outside the heavy metal doors, the leader of the Dalek security squad looked on in satisfaction as the cutting equipment gradually extended the glowing line. Another Dalek approached. On the end of its sucker arm was a crumpled scrap of paper. 'The dead Thal was carrying this paper.'

The squad leader studied the paper. It was the map Vaber had given Marat, after shifting the hiding-place of the explosives. 'It may contain information of importance. Send it to central control for analysis.'

'I obey.'

Inside the cooling chamber, the Doctor was showing the Thals how to tie lengths of rope to the corners of a huge square of plastic. 'I wish you'd tell us the point of all this,' grumbled Taron. 'Just what are we making?'

'Well, on Earth they'd call it a parachute—but it's a parachute for going up, not coming down. A parachute-balloon, say.'

'You're not trying to tell me we're going to fly up the chimney?' asked Codal incredulously.

'It's the only way we can get out,' said the Doctor. 'There's a powerful up-draft in that chimney. If we can trap a big enough pocket of it in this—all we have to do is hang on.'

Taron said, 'That's ridiculous, Doctor. It'll never work.'

'It had better,' the Doctor said grimly. 'Look!'

While they had been busy, the line on the door had

enlarged itself to form two sides of a square arch. Once the third side was cut, a huge chunk of the doors would simply fall away, leaving an arch through which Daleks could enter.

The knots completed, the Thals manhandled the unwieldy sheet of plastic across the room and began to stuff it up the cowling. They disappeared underneath, and after a moment Codal emerged. 'It's no good, Doctor. It's forming a pocket, but the updraft isn't strong enough.'

The Doctor rubbed his chin. 'Hold on, I'll switch the unit to maximum. That'll boost the updraft.'

The Doctor ran to the refrigeration unit and adjusted controls. Under the cowling, Taron and the others felt the updraft increase to a steady gale. The Doctor was crossing the room to join them when his attention was caught by something on the wall near by. A short ramp ran up to a little platform. Set in the wall just above the platform was a metal-shuttered window. The general effect was of a kind of viewing gallery. But a viewing gallery to what? Even under such dangerous circumstances as these, the Doctor was unable to resist it. Curiosity had always been his strongest characteristic. He ran up the ramp, pulled back the shutter and looked through.

From the other side of the room, Codal called, 'It's working, Doctor, the balloon's lifting.'

The Doctor scarcely heard. He was staring, in sheer amazement, at one of the most astonishing sights he had ever seen. The window looked out on to an enormous dimly lit cavern, metal catwalks round its walls. The cavern was so vast that its furthest walls were lost in shadow, and it was completely filled with row upon row of Daleks, thousands of them, rank after rank, standing completely still, wisps of icy vapour drifting about their bodies. A whole army of Daleks, silent, motionless, waiting...

Another shout from Codal broke into the Doctor's trance. 'Doctor, they're nearly through. Hurry!'

The Doctor looked at the metal doors. The third side of the arch was almost cut through. He ran to the cowling. The plastic 'parachute' had risen far up the chimney, and the Thals were hanging on to the ropes. Taron tossed one to the Doctor and he caught hold, wrapping it round his fists. The ropes were tugging hard now, trying to lift them up but not quite making it. The Dalek cutting machine was on the last few inches of the arch. 'It's no use,' yelled Codal. 'There's not enough lift to take all our weights.'

'Give it time,' said the Doctor steadily. 'It'll take us up.'

'It isn't going to work,' said Rebec desperately.

The leader of the Dalek security squad watched the cutting machine complete the last section of its arch. A Dalek gripped the cutaway section with a magnetic clamp and pulled. The section lifted out, and the Dalek pulled it clear, leaving a cut-out archway in the metal doors.

'Attack force prepare,' ordered the squad leader. 'Maximum fire power. All prisoners to be exterminated.'

Gun sticks at the ready, the Daleks swept into the cooling chamber.

# 7
## Ascent to Peril

The cooling chamber was empty.

The astonishment of the Daleks was almost ludicrous. They crowded into the room, spinning round wildly in search of the fugitives. There was a note of hysteria in the leader's voice. 'Escape from this section is impossible. There are no other exits. The prisoners are hiding. Locate and destroy. They are to be exterminated.'

The orders *sounded* logical but they were impossible to carry out. There was nowhere for the prisoners to hide, nowhere to search. The Daleks milled about the room in a state of utter confusion.

The Doctor and his friends meanwhile were floating slowly up the great metal chimney, the plastic sheet billowing above them like the sail of some great yacht. As the doors finally gave way they had achieved lift-off, disappearing up the chimney seconds before the Daleks had entered the room. Once they were under way the ascent seemed to go easier, and now they were rising slowly but surely upwards. Quite a pleasant sensation, the Doctor was thinking. He really must try hot-air ballooning some time.

Rebec glanced down and shivered, closing her eyes. 'How far have we climbed?'

The Doctor looked at the drop beneath them. 'Hard to tell. I just hope we're high enough to be out of range. One of them's bound to look up here sooner or later.'

Even as the Doctor was speaking, a Dalek had glided beneath the cowling. Its eye-stalk swivelled casually upwards, then it let out an astonished squawk. 'Prisoners located.' It raised its gun-stick and fired.

They heard the roar of the blast as it echoed round the chimney, and even felt the heat, but they were quite unharmed. 'That's a relief,' said the Doctor. 'It seems we *are* out of range!' He saw Rebec twisting on her rope, sobbing with fear. 'Just keep your eyes closed, my dear, and hang on tight. You'll be all right.'

He looked at the two others. Taron was hanging on in grim silence, but Codal was looking about him keenly, scientific interest overcoming his fears. 'How long before we get to the top, Doctor?'

'Quite a while. We're coming right up from the lowest level, remember. It's going to be a long, slow climb.'

In the cooling chamber below, the Dalek leader was giving orders to retrieve the situation. 'A patrol will be sent to the surface immediately, to the point where the shaft emerges. They must reach the area before the prisoners can escape. Order an anti-gravitational disc to be brought here immediately.'

'I obey.' The second-in-command glided from the room. The leader moved under the cowling and swivelled his eye-stalk upwards.

The prisoners were scarcely visible now, just slowly

ascending dots. But they had not escaped. Soon Daleks would be waiting at the head of the chimney, and a Dalek pursing them up it. They had simply entered a trap, with no escape.


Jo Grant wondered if she was doomed to spend the rest of her life hiding in Dalek control like a rat in the wainscotting. There was only one Dalek in the area now, but it was still too near her. Her heart sank when two more entered and crossed to 'her' Dalek. 'You will come with us. The ice eruption is under control. We have discovered where the Thals have hidden their explosives. We must find and destroy them.' The new arrival carried a crumpled scrap of paper on its sucker-arm. Although Jo did not know it, this was the map taken from Marat's body.

'I obey.' The three Daleks left the control room—and the way to Jo's escape was clear. After a moment's reflection, she decided to follow the patrol. For one thing, they would presumably lead her out of the city. For another, perhaps she would find some way of preventing them from finding the Thal explosives. There was no way she could help the Doctor directly, now; the next best thing was to help the Thals.

Jo slipped along the corridor after the three Daleks. They passed the laboratory area where slave Spiridons were still unloading endless baskets of vegetation. Tossed over a crate, Jo saw one of the voluminous fur robes worn by the Spiridons. Presumably its invisible owner had abandoned it in defiance of regulations. Hoping he was nowhere near, Jo snatched up the robe and pulled it on. Grabbing an empty basket, she set off boldly after the Dalek patrol.

The robe was far too big, but that was all to the good. It covered her entire body from head to foot, and the loose sleeves concealed her hands. It didn't seem to bother the Daleks that they were being trailed by a very small Spiridon. Presumably Spiridon slaves were beneath their notice.

Jo followed the patrol along the corridors, into the lift, up to the surface and out into the jungle, without being stopped or checked. As soon as she was clear of the blockhouse, she dropped behind the patrol and dumped her disguise and the empty basket in a clump of bushes. Using the jungle for cover, she hurried after them.

The Daleks led her through the jungle across an area of rocky hillside, and finally into a sort of quarry. Watching from a distance, Jo felt the ground beneath her vibrating. She could see the Daleks moving to and fro along the bottom of the quarry, a rock wall rearing up above them like a cliff-face. The rock was loose and crumbly. Occasionally chunks rattled down on to the patrol, dislodged by subterranean vibrations from the icecano. Eventually one of the Daleks paused by a large rock. The others joined it, and between them they pushed the rock away, revealing the entrance to a tiny cave. Inside the cave mouth lay a plastic bundle.

Jo crept closer, until she was near enough to hear what the Daleks were saying. 'Explosives are equipped with detonating mechanisms. We will explode them here. Activate mechanisms.' One of the Daleks glided closer to the bomb cache, its sucker arm reaching out. 'All mechanisms now primed. The bombs will self-detonate when we have left the area. We shall return to the city and assist in recapturing the escaped prisoners.'

The three Daleks wheeled and filed away. Jo waited until they were out of sight, then made her way towards the bombs. Acting on the general principle that whatever the Daleks wanted, she was against, Jo was determined to switch off the bombs if she possibly could. Maybe the Thals or the Doctor would get a chance to pick them up later and use them against the Daleks.

The bombs lay in the cave mouth, ticking away quietly. They were stubby metal cylinders, silvery in colour, each surmounted with a small clock face. The single hand on each clock was moving slowly from the 'one o'clock' to the 'twelve o'clock' position. It was easy enough to work out that when the hand reached twelve the bombs would blow up. Beside the clock face was a button, like that on a stop watch. Bracing herself, Jo reached out and pressed the button. The hand stopped moving. She gave a sigh of relief and switched off the second bomb, ignoring the dirt and small stones rattling down from overhead.

A further shower rained down as Jo moved over to the third bomb. Unfortunately this contained a few larger stones, and one of them struck Jo behind the ear as she leaned over the third bomb. It wasn't very big, only slightly larger than a tennis ball, but the impact was enough to knock her out. She slumped forward over the third bomb. Since she hadn't managed to turn it off, this third bomb was still ticking. The hand on its clock moved steadily towards detonation point.


Dangling from their parachute-balloon, the Doctor and the Thals were now near the top of the enormous chimney. The round disc of blue sky was getting bigger and nearer, and they were beginning to hope they might actually reach it. The Doctor seemed to be enjoying himself. 'You must admit,' he said chattily, 'it really is rather an exhilarating sensation.'

Rebec, her eyes tight shut, spoke through clenched teeth. 'The only time I ever want to leave the ground again, is in the rocket that takes me away from this planet.'

'Now don't *worry*,' said the Doctor reassuringly. 'As long as you hold on tight, you're perfectly safe.'

Above the Doctor's head, at the point where his rope was attached to the plastic sheeting, a tiny tear had appeared. Slowly, very slowly, it began to spread.

A long way below, in the cooling chamber at the bottom of the chimney, a squad of Daleks was manoeuvring a flat metal disc into position beneath the cowling. It was about a foot thick, and just big enough for one Dalek to stand securely in the centre. The squad leader glided up a little ramp and took his position on the disc. A Dalek scientist reported, 'Antigravitational disc now in position. Energy building up to full lift-off capacity.'

Even as he spoke, a hum of power came from within the disc. It built up to a throbbing crescendo and then stopped. The squad leader ordered, 'Prepare for lift-off!'

The energy hum started again, this time with a steady throbbing note. 'Lift-off!'

The anti-gravitational disc rose slowly in the air, carrying the Dalek up the long chimney in pursuit of the fugitives.

Meanwhile, another Dalek patrol was moving swiftly through the jungle on its way to intercept the prisoners at the top of the shaft. A report from central control had informed them that the prisoners were still in the chimney, and they were confident of arriving in time to exterminate them as they emerged. The patrol's route took it into the rocky area where the hills rose out of the jungle. They were passing along a trail that led through a kind of quarry when their leader spotted a suspicious sight on the rock slope ahead. A small figure was crouching over some silvery objects. The patrol leader halted. 'We have discovered a Thal saboteur with hidden explosives. The Thal must be captured and interrogated.' They began gliding along the path towards the cave.

Jo Grant was just recovering consciousness. Muzzily she climbed to her hands and knees, shaking her head to clear it. Suddenly she became aware of double danger. The clock-hand on the third bomb had almost reached detonation point. And several Daleks were advancing towards her along the trail.

Jo grabbed the two switched-off bombs and scrambled up the rocky slope. The Daleks increased their pace. 'Halt. Halt and surrender or you will be exterminated!'

Ignoring the order Jo stumbled on. The Daleks followed after, confident they could stun her with their blasters when they were close enough.

As the Dalek patrol came level with the little cave, the third bomb exploded. There was a tremendous explosion and a huge avalanche of earth and rocks poured down. Jo flung herself to the ground, still clasping the two bombs. Earth and stones rumbled past her, but this time her luck was better, and she survived unharmed. When the noise died away she looked up.

Where the Daleks had been was a huge pile of rubble, burying them completely. A bomb under each arm, Jo stumbled towards the shelter of the jungle.

The parachute–balloon had almost reached the top of the shaft by now. The Doctor peered upwards. 'The chimney narrows near the top and the sides are ribbed. The parachute may jam, but we should be able to climb up. Be ready to grab a hand-hold.'

Taron was looking downwards. 'There's something coming up after us!'

The Doctor glanced down and saw the tiny dot of the anti-gravitational disc moving steadily up the chimney. 'It's all right,' he called. 'It isn't climbing any faster than we are—and we've got a big start. We'll be at the top before it gets in range.'

Suddenly he heard Rebec scream, 'Look, Doctor, the parachute! It's tearing!'

The little tear by the Doctor's rope had become a huge rip, spreading rapidly across the plastic sheeting. 'The whole thing's going,' he yelled. 'Jump for the sides—we'll have to climb.' One by one, Rebec, Codal and Taron jumped for the metal ribbing, scaling it like a ladder. They climbed up and up, arms and legs aching, for what seemed an incredibly long way. At last, one by one, they were able to scramble over a low stone parapet that bordered the chimney outlet and into the open air. Taron was the last to climb out. He leaned over the parapet and looked down the chimney. 'The Doctor's still inside!' he yelled.

Last to leave the falling balloon, the Doctor had succeeded only in catching the very lowest rung of the ribbing ladder. With no foothold to help him climb, he was dangling from it by both hands.

Lower down the chimney, the crumpled mass of plastic, its supporting air-pocket dispersed, was drifting slowly downwards.

Lower still, the anti-gravitational disc, the Dalek passenger clearly visible by now, rose steadily towards the helpless Doctor.

# 8

# The Enemy Within

Swiftly Taron uncoiled the length of plastic rope from his shoulder and lowered it into the shaft. It was almost long enough, but not quite. The end of the rope dangled less than a foot from the Doctor's hands. He gave a worried glance below him. The Dalek on its anti-gravitational disc was rising steadily higher. It would soon be near enough to fire. The falling plastic threatened to smother it, and the Dalek blasted it into flaming fragments.

At the top of the shaft Taron called, 'He can't reach it. Rebec, Codal, hold my legs.' He lowered the upper half of his body into the shaft, straining to bring the rope within the Doctor's grasp. Taron stretched dangerously forward, the Doctor let go with one hand and reached out—and the end of the rope brushed the tips of his fingers.

The pursuing Dalek was very close now. The rescuers made one final effort. Taron leaned full-length into the shaft, secured only by Codal and Rebec's grip on his ankles. The Doctor lunged desperately upwards and managed to catch the end of the rope with his left hand. Just as he did so, his right slipped from the smooth metal of the ribbing. He dangled spinning in mid-air, clasping the rope with one hand.

Rebec and Codal gripped Taron's legs, helping to brace him against the Doctor's weight on the rope. The Doctor, meanwhile, grabbed the rope with his other hand, and started to climb it hand over hand, even as the three Thals were pulling it up. Taron fell back outside the parapet, then the Doctor shot out of the chimney like a cork out of a bottle, and scrambled over the parapet.

'Dalek,' he gasped. 'Still coming up.' He looked round for a weapon. Embedded in the ground near the parapet was a huge round boulder. The Doctor ran to it and started heaving with his shoulder. The boulder tilted a little. 'All of you, help me,' he ordered. Even with four of them it was a tremendous effort to roll the boulder up the hillside and then to lift it up on to the parapet. Heaving and panting they managed it at last. For a moment the boulder was poised on the parapet. Then the Doctor yelled, 'Heave!', and with a final shove, they tipped it over.

They crowded round the parapet to see the result. The boulder whistled down the shaft and struck the disc's edge, spinning it like a coin and wrecking the anti-gravitational mechanism. Boulder, disc and Dalek tumbled down the shaft together, gathering speed as they fell.

At the bottom of the shaft the squad of Daleks was gathered round waiting. The hurling objects shot out of the shaft all together. There was a tremendous roar as the disc exploded, and the Daleks were blown in all directions.

At the top of the chimney, the Doctor and his friends heard the noise. The Doctor smiled in satisfaction. 'That should hold them for a while. Let's get away from here, before their patrol arrives.'

Taron said, 'We must get to the quarry where Vaber left the explosives. If the Daleks find that map they'll try to destroy them.'

They set off down the hillside. As they were approaching the quarry, Jo Grant was leaving it. She met them crossing a jungle clearing.

Scarcely able to believe her eyes, Jo flung herself into the Doctor's arms. 'Doctor, I thought you were still in the TARDIS. I thought you were dying ... oh I don't know *what* I thought.'

The Doctor was just as delighted, and even more surprised. 'But I thought *you* were dead. I thought you were in that Thal spaceship when the Daleks blew it up...'

Jo began pouring out a confused account of her adventures, but the Doctor stopped her. 'There'll be plenty of time for explanations later. You've already met Taron and Codal. This is Rebec.'

Jo gave them a polite hello, and turned back to the Doctor. 'I heard you'd been taken prisoner by the Daleks. I went into the city to rescue you...'

'You did what?'

Taron interrupted them. 'It'll be dark soon. I think we'd better pick up those explosives.'

'If you're talking about some bombs hidden in a quarry—don't bother,' said Jo. 'One of them went off, and I've hidden the others in a clearing nearby.' She told them what had happened at the quarry.

Taron shook his head wearily. 'So much has been going on that it's hard to think straight. We'd better rest here for a while.'

The Thals set up camp. Their seemingly inexhaustible back-packs produced supplies of concentrated food, and tiny atomic-powered stoves with which to heat it. Soon they were all washing down the tough, chewy food-concentrates with delicious hot soup, and Jo felt strength flooding back into her body. As they ate, Jo and the Doctor brought each other up to date on their mutual adventures. Both realised how lucky they were to have come together again unharmed.

The Doctor took a swig of soup. 'But why didn't you just stay inside the TARDIS, Jo? We'd have been safe there—while the air lasted.'

'You didn't *look* very safe. I thought you were dying, so I went to find help.'

'On a planet occupied by the Daleks? Surely I warned you.'

'You didn't warn me about anything, Doctor. You rushed into the TARDIS, rattled off a quick telepathic telegram to the Time Lords and then collapsed.'

The Doctor looked crestfallen. 'I'm sorry, Jo. I wasn't quite myself! I asked the Time Lords to send us after the Daleks, then I blacked out.'

'What are the Daleks doing on this planet, anyway?'

'I *thought* they were just studying the secret of invisibility, but there's more to it than that. They've got an enormous army concealed here, I saw it myself. It's obviously part of some plan to conquer the Galaxy ...'

While the Doctor and Jo were talking, Rebec and Taron sat together near by. It was their first chance to be alone since they had met again on this planet. Back home on Skaro they had been close friends, with an understanding that they would eventually marry. But here on Spiridon, Rebec had found Taron a different man, his manner strained and almost hostile. 'You might at least say you're glad to see me,' she said lightly.

He looked coldly at her. 'I might. Why did you come?'

'Because I wanted to be with you.'

Taron was silent for a moment, then he burst out, 'Don't you understand what you've done? Even if Vaber and Latep are alive, there are still only five of us. Five survivors from two missions, to destroy an army of Daleks.'

'How does my being here make things any worse?'

In a level voice Taron said, 'Because I love you. And that will cloud my judgement. I may hesitate to take risks, necessary risks, because I'll be worrying about you. And if my judgement fails, then the Daleks will win!' He got quickly to his feet and crossed to the other side of the clearing. Rebec began sobbing quietly to herself.

The Doctor looked up from his conversation with Jo. As always he was very well aware of what was going on around him. Casually he got up. 'I think I'll have a quick word with Taron. Rebec might appreciate a feminine shoulder at the moment.'

While Jo went to console Rebec, the Doctor joined Taron on the other side of the clearing. He was staring morosely into the thick green jungle, its leafy depths shadowed with the approaching darkness. 'Load getting a bit heavy, old chap?' asked the Doctor.

Taron couldn't help responding to the sympathy in his voice. 'I'm not sure I can handle things any more.'

'Because you're not made of stone?'

'I have to *lead* this expedition, Doctor. It's a job that doesn't allow for human weakness.'

'Perhaps they should have sent a machine.'

'I thought I could act like one,' said Taron grimly. 'I was wrong.'

'Good!' said the Doctor heartily. 'The business of command is not meant for machines. Forget you're dealing with people's lives and you're no better than the creatures we came to destroy. Once *we* start acting like Daleks—the battle's already lost!'

Taron was about to reply when he heard movement in the jungle. He drew his blaster and waited, calling a warning to the others. 'Look out, someone's coming.' They waited tensely—and Vaber and Latep came out of the jungle. There was a joyful reunion among the Thals. Vaber and Latep had been about half-way along their chosen ice-fissure when they had heard the icecano beginning to erupt. Not daring to go on they had set their bombs to explode, only to see them engulfed by a surge of ice which had absorbed the effects of the explosion. 'We were lucky to get clear alive,' concluded Latep. 'We went to the quarry to get the other bombs, but they'd already been exploded.'

Jo couldn't resist joining in. 'Not all of them. I

rescued two and buried them not far away.'

'Then we've still got a chance,' said Vaber eagerly. 'We can attack again in the morning.'

'Maybe,' said Taron, 'but meanwhile we've got to get through the night. We can't stay here, it's too near the main Dalek trails. Besides, we'd never survive the cold. We'll have to go to the Plain of Stones.'

The Doctor looked puzzled. Codal came forward and explained. 'It's an area scattered with huge boulders. They're made of a stone that soaks up the sun's heat during the day and releases it at night.'

'Sort of night storage heaters,' suggested Jo. 'It'll be nice to be somewhere warm for the night.'

'It's a dangerous place,' warned Codal. 'A lot of wild animals go there for the warmth.'

Taron said, 'Jo, will you take Latep to the place where you hid the bombs? The rest of us will pack up camp.'

Jo turned to Latep, who smiled at her. She decided she quite liked the look of him. He had a cheerful open face, and as the youngest and smallest of the Thals, he was the only one anywhere near her own age and size. All the rest of them towered over her, and seemed terribly serious about everything. Jo held out her hand. Latep looked at it in amazement. She realised he didn't know what she meant. 'It's an old Earth custom,' she explained. 'We clasp hands like this to show we're pleased to meet each other.'

Latep took her hand and shook it vigorously. 'Come on,' said Jo. 'Let's go and get those bombs.'

With the bombs collected and the camp packed

up, they all set off through the jungle again. It was almost dark now, and getting very cold. Codal was moving ahead of the main group, acting as scout. Suddenly he called back, 'Down everybody! It's a Dalek patrol.'

The Doctor dropped to the ground, and wriggled forward on his elbows to lie beside Codal. On the trail just ahead, a Dalek patrol was gliding through the dusk. Accompanying them were Spiridons in their furry, all-concealing robes.

As the patrol disappeared into the darkness, the Doctor tapped Codal on the shoulder. 'Did you notice how slowly that patrol was moving? Almost as though their reflexes weren't functioning properly.'

Taron joined them. 'They're still fast enough to kill us on sight, Doctor. I think we can chance moving on now.'

An indignant voice floated forward to them. 'Let's get on with it then, I'm freezing!' It was Jo. Taron waved them on, and they all moved forward.

The Plain of Stones was exactly what its name suggested, a bleak plain littered with huge boulders. Their fantastic, twisted shapes loomed up out of the darkness. From all around came the growling, chattering and howling of Spiridon animal life. They found a circle of boulders grouped together, a kind of miniature Stonehenge, and decided to make camp between them. As they were settling down, there came a sudden hoarse scream, and a great black shape swooped over their heads, with a flapping of enormous wings. Jo gripped Latep's arm. 'What was that?' The boy shrugged and it was Taron who answered.

'Some kind of pterodactyl, I think. They only come out at night.' He turned to the Doctor. 'Will you take the first guard with Latep, Doctor?'

'Yes, of course. Maybe you'll keep us company for a while, Jo?'

They became aware of angry voices. Vaber was helping Codal to set up camp, and indulging in his usual complaints. Since the failure of the attack on the Dalek city, his old moroseness had returned. 'I'm sick of all this running and hiding, Codal,' he was saying. 'We need to attack, and soon.'

Taron crossed over to them. 'I'll decide that, Vaber.'

'You—you've already bungled one attack. You missed your greatest opportunity.'

Taron sighed. 'And what was that?'

'The refrigeration plant. Codal's been telling me about it. Obviously it's vital to the success of the Daleks' plans.'

'We still don't know *why* the Daleks need such low temperatures,' said Taron mildly.

'Who cares about *why*? The fact is they do. Destroy that refrigeration plant and we ruin the Daleks' plans. We can go back down the shaft you came up. Better still we could just lower the bombs down...'

Taron shook his head. 'The Daleks won't have left that shaft unguarded. We'll attack again, but the whole thing has to be properly planned. Until then, we wait.'

The word might have been chosen to enrage Vaber. 'Wait!' he sneered. 'That's all we hear from you. I suppose you're scared to take any action with her round your neck.' He nodded towards Rebec, who was standing listening to the argument in distress.

Taron's big hands flashed out and gripped Vaber round the throat, shaking him savagely. Vaber kicked Taron's feet from under him, and the two men rolled struggling on the ground. The Doctor's voice cracked out like a whip. 'Stop that, both of you. Get up at once!'

Shamefacedly the two Thals got to their feet. For all their size and strength they looked like children caught brawling in the playground. The Doctor spoke more gently. 'We'll never defeat the Daleks unless we stay united. We're letting the strain make us suspicious and hostile. That's the real enemy, the enemy within. Not the Daleks but our own fears.'

For a long moment Taron and Vaber glared at each other. Then Taron said slowly, 'I'm still in command here, Vaber. We'll attack when I say so, and not before. Like it or not, you'll obey orders. If you don't— I'll kill you!'


In the control room, the Dalek Expedition Commander was addressing his aides. Grouped around him in a semi-circle, they listened meekly to the arrogant voice. 'One Patrol is missing. Others report no contact with the prisoners. Supreme Command are gravely displeased with the progress of this operation.' No one replied, or attempted excuses. The Expedition Commander went on, 'Supreme Command has decreed we prepare a bacteriological weapon. It will destroy all living tissue on Spiridon. Daleks and

Spiridon slave workers will be given immunity to the disease.'

Again there was no reply. It did not occur to any Dalek to protest at this ruthless proposal to wipe out the life-forms of an entire planet. Massive retaliation to opposition had always been the Dalek way. The Commander turned to a Dalek Scientist. 'Report progress on the bacteriological weapon.'

The Dalek Scientist indicated a metal trolley inside the laboratory. Through the glass wall they could see that it contained a number of jars. 'The bacteria are now multiplying. After release into the atmosphere, the culture will totally contaminate the planet. All plant life will wither and die. All un-immunised animal life will be exterminated. The culture will be ready for release in one Spiridon day.'

'Approved. Continue preparations.'

Another Dalek entered and stood waiting to speak. The Commander swung towards it. 'Report.'

'Spiridon slave-spies report aliens in hiding at Plain of Stones.'

'Order all search units to concentrate on that area.'

'I obey.'


Her back against one of the boulders, Jo Grant was dozing comfortably. The huge rock gave out a steady warm glow, and she was having a confused dream about holidays on the French Riviera. Gradually she became aware of an agitated voice, breaking into her dream and bringing her awake. It was Taron, shaking the Doctor who lay dozing beside her. 'Doctor, wake up. It's Vaber. He's cleared off and taken the bombs. He left this note.'

Taron held out the note and the Doctor read it aloud. 'I'll do what has to be done on my own.' He tossed the note back to Taron. 'Of all the melodramatic nonsense. He doesn't stand a chance on his own.'

'Neither do we now,' said Taron grimly. 'He's taken the last of the explosives. I'm going after him.'

The Doctor rose. 'I'll come with you.'

'I'd prefer you to take charge here.'

The Doctor was pleased by Taron's trust. 'All right. If that's what you want.'

'Codal, you come with me,' ordered Taron. 'The rest of you stay here. The Doctor's in command till I get back.'

Codal and Taron slipped away into the darkness. Jo drifted back to sleep, only to be awakened by the Doctor. 'I think we'd better build a fire,' he said.

Jo was still drowsy, disinclined to move. 'Why, Doctor? It's warm enough with these boulders.'

'Not for warmth, Jo, for safety. Look!' The Doctor pointed. A circle of fiercely glowing eyes ringed the camp. The wild-life of Spiridon was moving in for the kill.


Vaber didn't stand a chance. A bomb clutched under each arm, he stumbled towards the Dalek city, blind to everything except the need to justify himself against Taron—Taron who'd taken away the command that was rightfully his own. A bulky shape loomed out of the darkness—a fur-clad Spiridon. Vaber turned to run, but other shapes surrounded him. They threw themselves upon him, and claw-like hands gripped him so that he could not move. He heard a throaty whisper. 'Take him to the Daleks!'

# 9
## Vaber's Sacrifice

Hiding nearby in the jungle, Taron and Codal
looked on appalled. They had been close behind
Vaber, about to seize him themselves and recover the
bombs, when they had witnessed his capture by the
Spiridon patrol. There was no chance of a rescue. The
Spiridons were too numerous. The two Thals
watched helplessly as Vaber was hurried away. Taron
tapped Codal's shoulder. 'We've got to recover those
bombs. Come on.' Silently they began to follow the
Spiridons and their prisoner.


The Doctor, Jo, Rebec and Latep huddled around
the little fire. Already it had proved a problem to
keep it going. There wasn't much fuel in the immediate area, and to go out into the darkness would have
brought them within range of the creatures with the
glowing eyes. Despite the fire, those eyes seemed to be
moving closer. Rebec drew her blaster. 'I'll try a shot
at them.' She fired at random into the darkness.
There was a crackle of energy and a howl of pain.
The eyes retreated. Then after a moment they returned, creeping even closer.

'They don't stay scared for long, do they?' the
Doctor said grimly.

Rebec fired again. This time the energy-crackle suddenly fizzled out. 'The charge is exhausted.' she explained.

The Doctor looked at Latep who shook his head. 'I'm sorry—I lost my blaster in the crash.'

The Doctor sighed. 'We'd better find more wood for the fire.' They began to search. Behind one of the nearby boulders the Doctor found a kind of stunted tree. Wrenching it from the thin soil, he carried it over to the fire. 'This should keep us going for a time.' While the others broke off twigs and threw them on the fire, the Doctor trimmed a couple of larger branches to use as clubs. He lit the end of one in the fire and advanced towards the threatening eyes, waving the blazing torch in front of him. With angry roars the unseen creatures retreated. 'Get yourselves torches, all of you,' he ordered. Jo and the others obeyed, and a vigorous advance with blazing branches soon sent the creatures scurrying away. 'They'll come back of course,' said the Doctor cheerfully. 'But at least we've given ourselves a respite.'

Exhausted by their efforts, they sat silently round the fire. Eventually the Doctor said, 'What possessed Vaber to go rushing off like that?'

Rebec sighed. 'Once he'd worked out his plan, he couldn't bear to wait.'

'What plan?'

'To blow up the Dalek refrigeration unit. He thought if he destroyed that, he'd destroy the Daleks.'

The Doctor looked at her in horror. 'On the contrary—he'd be bringing their army to life.'

'Doctor,' said Jo, 'if you'd only remember to *ex-*

*plain* things occasionally . . .'

The Doctor took a deep breath. 'All right, I will. The Daleks I saw in that arsenal-place, next to the cooling chamber, were in a state of suspended animation. No ageing process, no degeneration, no maintenance needed. An *army* of Daleks, in cold storage until it's needed. *That's* why the Daleks came to this planet. To use it as a base. The invisibility business is only a side-line. What they were really after was the planet's core of ice. But they found the icecano was too unstable, so they built the refrigeration unit.' He looked round at the others. 'The minute the temperature rises, all those Daleks will come to life.' He was interrupted by a hoarse voice from the darkness.

'Jo! I have found you.'

The Doctor leaped to his feet. A bulky figure moved into the circle of firelight, fur-clad and carrying an ugly-looking club. The Doctor grabbed for a club of his own, but Jo spoke up, 'It's all right, Doctor. It's Wester—the Spiridon who helped me when I was ill.'

The Doctor lowered his club. 'Then I owe you a great debt. Please accept my thanks.' He held out his hand and felt it gripped by another invisible one, emerging from the wide sleeve of the furs.

The whispering voice said, 'I have news from the city. The Daleks have prepared a bacteriological weapon. It will destroy all life on this planet, except for the Daleks and their servants. I wanted to warn you. Now I shall go back to the city to try and prevent them.'

The Doctor's voice was grave. 'We'll do all we can

to help. Thank you for warning us.'

Jo started to say, 'Wester, be careful...' But the Spiridon had already vanished.

The Doctor said decisively, 'We'll move out at full light.'

'What about Taron and the others?' Rebec protested.

'We'll wait till dawn. If they're not back by then—we must go without them.'


The Spiridon patrol moved swiftly down the trail. A nucleus of them stayed tightly clustered around their prisoner. Others ranged in a wider group, acting as scouts and rearguards. The last Spiridon of the patrol was some way behind the others. The patrol heard nothing as suddenly Codal and Taron leaped from hiding and bore the rearguard Spiridon to the ground, stunning him with swift blows. Taron stripped the fur robes from the invisible creature and pulled them on himself. 'I'll try to get close to Vaber,' he whispered. 'Be ready to move in when I jump the guards.'

Codal nodded, and Taron ran to join the rest of the patrol. Codal followed at a distance, keeping under cover.

Taron caught up with the patrol, indistinguishable from the Spiridons in his furs. The patrol moved on for quite some way, and still Taron made no move. Codal began to worry. Surely they'd be at the Dalek city before very long. Dodging through a clump of bushes he crept closer to the last figure in the patrol, tapping it on the shoulder. 'Taron,' he whispered, 'surely it's time we...' The figure swung round. To his horror Codal saw there was no face beneath the hood, just emptiness. He was talking to a genuine Spiridon.

The creature jumped him, invisible hands reaching out. Codal struggled desperately but the Spiridon was very strong. Suddenly his opponent jerked and went limp. Yet another fur-clad figure had appeared and stunned it, and this one *was* Taron. 'What do you think you're doing?' he whispered angrily.

Codal laughed hysterically. 'I *spoke* to him. I thought he was you!'

'Nearly got yourself killed,' muttered Taron. 'Still, it's provided us with another disguise. Get these furs on and follow me. I've marked out the one carrying the bombs. When I jump him, you grab the bombs and run. They're first priority.'

'What about you?'

'As soon as you're away I'll free Vaber. We'll make a run for it.'

Codal nodded, glad they were not abandoning Vaber, despite all the trouble he had caused them. Soon two fur-clad figures were hurrying to rejoin the Spiridon patrol.

Taron was just about to make his move when ill-fortune struck. The Spiridons encountered a patrol of Daleks, and came to an immediate full stop. A Dalek voice rasped, 'Halt. What is happening?'

Eager for praise, a Spiridon whispered, 'We have captured one of the aliens. He was carrying explosives.' The Dalek patrol leader glided forward to where Vaber was held by two Spiridons.

'Where are your fellow Thals hiding?'

Vaber's voice was defiant. 'No idea. You want them, you find them.'

'Release him. Move away.' The Spiridons holding Vaber let go and stepped back. The Dalek's gun-stick swung to cover Vaber's isolated figure. 'Answer or I will exterminate you.'

Vaber seemed to wilt beneath the threat. 'No ... don't fire. I'll take you to them...'

There was satisfaction in the Dalek's voice. 'We will start at once.'

Vaber turned as if to lead the way. Suddenly he ducked between the two Spiridons and sprinted for the cover of the jungle. An outlying Spiridon grabbed him and they grappled desperately. Vaber managed to swing the Spiridon round, using him as a shield. But the death of one of their servants was of little concern to the Daleks. The patrol leader ordered, 'Open fire!' Dalek guns blazed and Vaber and the Spiridon were blasted down together.

As the Daleks moved towards the bodies, Taron and Codal acted. Moving in on the Spiridon with the bombs, they clubbed him to the ground, grabbed one bomb each and made off into the jungle. Confused by the flurry of movement the Daleks swung round and opened fire. But they were too late. Taron and Codal had disappeared. With angry cries of 'Pursue! Pursue and exterminate!' the Daleks followed after them.


A Dalek technician was reporting to the Chief Scientist. 'The antidote is prepared and ready to be administered.'

'Demonstrate.'

The technician produced a square, gun-shaped device mounted on a trolley, and touched a control. There was a fierce hiss and a fine cloud of mist covered them both. 'Synthesised anti-bacteriological elements have been released. The elements provide immunity on contact.'

'Approved. I will order all Dalek units and Spiridon slave workers to assemble for treatment. Are the bacteria now ready for release?'

Proudly the Dalek technician gestured towards the other trolley. 'The growth process is complete. Removal of the container tops is all that is required to allow bacteria to enter the atmosphere.'

Dawn came at last, with a sudden blaze of light and heat. Thankfully the Doctor let the fire die down. The creatures of Spiridon had returned to their lairs. The Doctor disappeared on a brief scouting expedition, while Latep scanned the plain from on top of a high rock. Jo heard him call out, 'Someone's coming. It's Codal and Taron!' Codal and Taron hurried into camp, the Doctor close behind them.

There was time only for the quickest of reunions. A saddened silence fell as Taron told them of Vaber's fate. The Doctor said, 'He was rash and impulsive, poor fellow, but he was right about one thing. It *is* time we went over to the attack.'

Defensively Taron said, 'If you can provide me with a *workable* plan...'

'I think I can,' the Doctor said gently. 'I've been thinking it out for most of the night. Will you trust me?'

Taron nodded wearily. 'I'll leave it to you, Doctor. You can't do worse than I've done.'

'Nonsense,' said the Doctor briskly. 'We gathered invaluable information on that first attack. Now it's time to put our knowledge to good use. We need to get back inside the city, undetected this time.'

'And how do we do that?'

'Well, the first thing we must do,' the Doctor said cheerfully, 'is to get ourselves spotted by a Dalek patrol!'

There was an astonished silence. The Doctor smiled, and added mysteriously, 'Come with me, will you, Taron? The rest of you wait here.'

The Doctor led Taron a little way into the hills that bordered the Plain of Stones. They stopped by a small round pool in the rocky ground. 'There!' announced the Doctor triumphantly. 'Found it this morning when I was having a scout around.'

Taron was unimpressed. 'The planet is full of these pools, Doctor. They're liquid ice, fed from the ice-cano.'

'Exactly. It's odd, but water on this planet seems to sustain sub-zero temperatures and still remain liquid.'

Taron said, 'I'm sorry, Doctor, but I *still* don't see...'

Patiently, the Doctor explained. 'Daleks are vulnerable to extremely low temperatures. At sub-zero levels, they wouldn't be able to function at all. *Now* do you see?'

A slow smile spread over Taron's face. 'Yes ... yes, I do see.' He started scanning the landscape around them. 'Let's look round and plan a way to make it work.'

The Doctor was smiling too. 'It's a good feeling, isn't it—when the hunted become the hunters?'

# 10

# Return to the City

After the death of the captured alien, and the escape of two others with their recovered bombs, the Dalek Commander ordered an intensified search of the Plain of Stones. The searchers worked in twos, not threes, to maximise the number of patrols. The leader of the first patrol knew that the aliens were cunning and desperate, and he was surprised when they found two of them almost immediately. Perhaps tiredness was making them careless.

The two aliens, both young and small, were standing in the middle of the track that led to the Plain of Stones, almost as if they *wanted* to be seen. When the patrol spotted them, they turned and ran off between the rocks. They moved slowly, as if very tired, and the patrol soon began to overhaul them. 'Pursue and exterminate,' ordered the patrol leader. 'Supreme Command advise no prisoners to be taken. They must be exterminated!'

The aliens disappeared once they were among the rocks, and the Daleks were forced to hunt for them. Although there were only two of them, they moved confidently forward, quite sure of their ability to deal with aliens.

Jo and Latep collapsed panting behind a rock. 'Are

you all right, Jo?' gasped Latep.

'Just about. Never run so fast in my life!'

Latep peered from behind the rock. 'They're coming. Ready?' Jo nodded. They sprang from the rock and sprinted off.

The Daleks saw them and set off in pursuit.

Taron, Codal, Rebec and the Doctor were crouched behind a giant boulder beside the trail to the ice pool. The place was carefully chosen. The path was narrow here, and the Daleks would have to move in single file. Jo and Latep dashed along the path and joined them in hiding. Panting, Jo said, 'The Daleks are just behind us.'

'Right,' ordered the Doctor. 'Scatter, I'll take over.' Jo, Latep and Rebec took cover nearby. Taron and Codal ran down the trail to the pool, to their pre-arranged positions. The Doctor waited. When the two Daleks came in sight, he stepped from hiding, then instantly ducked back. Even so, he moved only just in time. The blast from a Dalek gun charred the rock above his head.

The patrol leader ordered, 'Give protective fire,' and moved off alone. The second Dalek followed more slowly, its gun-stick swivelling suspiciously all around.

The patrol leader rounded the boulder and moved cautiously along the trail that bordered the ice pool. Suddenly the Doctor appeared from behind one of the rocks, disappearing again almost immediately. The patrol leader moved forward. Another blast from its gun seared the rocks, very close to the Doctor. The Dalek was near to the edge of the pool now. Suddenly

Taron appeared from hiding. He charged the Dalek, gripping it from behind so the gun could not bear, and started shoving it by main force towards the ice pool. Circling behind the Dalek, the Doctor ran to help.

Slowly they edged it towards the pool. The Dalek resisted with all its strength. All the time it was calling, 'Assist! Assist! I am being attacked!'

Further down the trail, Jo saw the second Dalek speed forward to answer the call, and realised that she had to delay it. She dashed across the trail and the Dalek swung round in pursuit. Jo's foot turned on a small rock and she crashed to the ground, sprawled helplessly on the path as the Dalek bore down on her.

As the Dalek was about to fire, Latep jumped on it from the top of a near-by boulder. He had a Spiridon robe in his hands which he threw over the Dalek, covering the eye-stalk completely.

The Dalek spun round helplessly, shrieking, 'Vision circuits impaired. I am losing control.'

Somehow Latep stayed perched on top of the Dalek, holding the robe firmly in place. Codal ran from hiding, grabbed the Dalek's gun-stick and jammed it upwards, so that the blast of its firing exploded harmlessly in the air. Rebec and Jo came to help him, and between the three of them they shoved the helpless Dalek along the path taken by the patrol leader.

As they rounded the boulder, the Doctor and Taron gave the patrol leader a mighty shove that sent it splashing into the ice pool. The waters bubbled and hissed, and the leader's cries ended abruptly. The Doctor and Taron ran to help with the second Dalek.

Latep leaped from its back and joined them. Propelled by six pairs of arms, the Dalek shot off the path like a rocket and splashed into the ice pond beside its leader.

There was a chorus of shouts and hurrahs from the bank. Jo and the Doctor joined the jubilant Thals in an orgy of hand-shaking and back-slapping. Then the Doctor held up his hand for silence. 'Well done, all of you. But remember, we still have work to do!'

Taron and Latep switched on their heat units and waded into the icy water. 'Don't get directly in front of their guns,' warned the Doctor. 'They may still be dangerous. Pull the top sections clear.'

Taron and Latep did so, shuddering at the sight of the hideous creatures housed inside. 'Are they dead?' called the Doctor.

Latep swallowed as he answered, 'I think so. The cold must have killed them instantly.'

'You'll have to get the bodies out and throw them in the pond.'

Thankful for their thick space-gauntlets, Taron and Latep groped inside the machine-casing, and threw the twisted bodies into the pool. There was a general sigh of relief as they vanished beneath the surface. 'Now,' said the Doctor more cheerfully, 'let's get the machines on to the bank.'

They began heaving the machines out of the pond and on to the path.


A long file of Spiridon slave workers was moving slowly into the Dalek city, reporting for their immunisation treatments as ordered. No one noticed when Wester slipped from the jungle and joined the line. No one was concerned about one extra slave worker.

Inside the city a Dalek was waiting to direct them. 'Spiridon workers will proceed to level four to await treatment.' The file of docile slaves did as they were ordered. Except for Wester, who slipped away from the line and made his way towards the Dalek laboratory. He knew from other Spiridons in his resistance group that this was where the bacteria containers were being kept.

No one stopped him on his way there. There was a feeling of great excitement in the Dalek city, with Daleks bustling in all directions. But at the door to the control room, he was halted by a Dalek guard. 'Stop. What are you doing here?'

'I have a vital message for the Chief Scientist.'

'The Chief Scientist is occupied. You may enter the laboratory and report when he is free.' Scarcely able to believe his luck, Wester crossed the control area and waited by the sealed door to the laboratory. It hissed open to admit him, hissed closed behind him once he was inside.

Wester saw a group of Daleks gathered round a bulbous, gun-shaped device which was mounted on a metal trolley. Beside it on another trolley stood a number of transparent jars, their lids firmly sealed.

Wester made no attempt to approach the group of Daleks. Instead he slipped into the farthest corner of the laboratory. The Daleks seemed to be arguing among themselves.

The Chief Scientist asked angrily, 'Why are you not ready to administer the protective treatments as ordered?'

'There is a minor fault in the mechanism. I shall rectify it immediately.'

'Make all speed. Dalek units and Spiridon workers are assembled and waiting.'

The Dalek technicians clustered busily round the immunisation machine.

Wester slowly slipped the fur robes, symbol of slavery, from his body and stuffed them under a machine. Protected by his invisibility, the only weapon of his people, he waited for his opportunity.

Close to the entrance to the Dalek city an oddly assorted group was assembled. One Dalek, three fur-clad Spiridons, a Thal and a human female. Only the last two were actually what they seemed. Inside the machine casing of the Dalek crouched Rebec, ready to act as their passport into the city. The three Spiridons were Codal, Taron and the Doctor ... another unfortunate Spiridon had been ambushed to provide a third set of robes. The Doctor leaned towards the Dalek. 'Are you all right in there, Rebec?'

There came a muffled 'Yes' in reply. As the smallest, Jo would have been the logical choice to go inside the Dalek, but she had been so obviously unwilling that Rebec volunteered.

The Doctor turned to Jo and Latep. 'Are you sure you can find the right ventilation shaft?'

Latep nodded. 'Taron's given us a map.'

Jo said, 'I wish we could all go in together, Doctor.'

'A two-pronged attack doubles our chance of success. I want you to detonate your bomb in the tunnel near the cooling unit—but whatever you do, don't damage the unit itself. That must go on functioning.'

'We understand, Doctor.'

'Off you go then—and good luck!'

Jo and Latep moved away into the jungle. The Doctor looked anxiously after them for a moment, then gave Rebec's Dalek a hearty slap. A little jerkily she propelled it forward. The Doctor, Taron and Codal followed, three Spiridon slaves being escorted back to the city by their Dalek master. Codal hugged the remaining bomb, concealing it under his fur robes.

All went well until they reached the entrance itself. A Dalek guard glided forward to challenge them. 'All units were ordered back to base some time ago. You are late.'

Rebec's Dalek naturally enough said nothing. The guard spoke angrily. 'Report to central control immediately.' It moved aside, and all four entered the city.

When they emerged from the lift, it was easy enough to lose themselves in the general bustle of Daleks. There was a crowd assembled outside the control area, all with an air of expectant waiting. The Doctor and his party edged their way across until they were at a point where they could look through the glass wall into the sealed-off laboratory. They saw a small group of Daleks clustered round a trolley, apparently working on a gun-like device. Nearby stood another trolley, holding sealed containers.

'What are they doing?' whispered Taron.

'I imagine they're preparing to immunise this lot,' said the Doctor quietly. 'Those sealed jars must be the bacteria culture. If we can get close enough to the immunisation machine to wreck it, they won't be able to release the bacteria without killing themselves.' The Doctor became silent, trying to work out a feasible plan of attack.

The leading Dalek technician moved back from the immunisation-gun. 'Fault rectified. Equipment now fully operational.'

The Chief Scientist ordered, 'Start to administer protective treatment to all units immediately. When that is done, the jars of bacteria culture will be opened at selected points on the planet. All non-immunised life will be exterminated.'

The technician began pushing the trolley towards the door. Suddenly the immunisation-gun rose in the air of its own accord and crashed down on to the trolley of bacteria cultures, smashing most of the jars.

Taron gripped the Doctor's arm. 'There's an invisible Spiridon in there.'

'It's Wester,' said the Doctor, 'It must be. He said he was going to stop them. He's better qualified for sabotage than we are.'

By now there was pandemonium in the laboratory. Those jars still unsmashed were flying through the air, breaking open against the walls. The Dalek scientists milled about, trying to find their invisible opponent.

'He's released the bacteria while he's still in there,'

said Taron. 'He's committed suicide.'

The Doctor's voice was sad. 'I know. Listen!' The Dalek Chief Scientist was speaking over some kind of public address system. 'The door to this laboratory must never be opened. No one can enter. We can never leave here.'

'Don't you see?' whispered the Doctor. 'The Daleks still aren't immunised. If they open that hermetically sealed door, the bacteria will escape and destroy *them*. Wester's done our job for us, better than we ever could ... but it's cost him his life.'

Saddened they turned away. Daleks and Spiridons were milling about in confusion, and it wasn't difficult to slip away to a side corridor. 'We must find a lift and reach the lower levels,' ordered the Doctor.

They were almost up to the lift doors when a voice grated, 'Halt!' A Dalek had appeared at the end of the corridor. It glided towards them. 'Spiridon slave workers were ordered to wait on level four. Move!'

Rebec, inside her Dalek, stayed motionless. The Doctor, Taron and Codal huddled inside their furs, and slowly turned. As they came level with the Dalek it ordered, 'Wait!' Its eye-stick swivelled downwards. The Doctor followed the direction of its gaze. Taron's booted foot had emerged from his concealing robes. Suddenly the Dalek shrieked, 'You are not Spiridons. You are alien intruders. Emergency! Emergency! Emergency!'

## 11

# An Army Awakes

The Doctor made no attempt to bluff. He whipped off his furs, flung them over the Dalek's eye-stalk and gave it a shove that sent it reeling down the corridor. He and Taron grabbed Rebec's Dalek and shoved it along at full speed. Behind them they could hear a Dalek voice screeching out over the loudspeaker system. 'Alert! Alert! Alert! Aliens at liberty in city. Instigate maximum security conditions. Alert! Alert! Alert! Aliens accompanied by impostor Dalek. Find and exterminate!'

A Dalek patrol came round a corner to find itself facing two aliens, one each side of a Dalek. The aliens dodged back out of sight, but the Dalek did not move. Realising that this must be the impostor, the patrol opened fire.

The Dalek spun round, smoke and flames belching from its top-section. 'Impostor Dalek destroyed,' reported the patrol leader.

Just around the corner the Doctor, Taron, Codal and Rebec were running for their lives. The Doctor yelled to Rebec, 'You stopped being a Dalek just in time!' Rebec smiled back, too breathless to talk.

They found a lift at last and dashed inside. The Doctor adjusted the controls to take them directly to level zero. 'We've got to get to that arsenal,' he explained.

'Then what?' demanded Codal. 'You still haven't told us *all* your plan, Doctor. What use is one bomb against an army of Daleks?'

'A great deal of use—in the right place,' said the Doctor mysteriously. 'We can't destroy that army—but we *can* stop it ever going into action.'

The lift door opened and they emerged on the lowest level. They ran to the cooling section from which they had escaped such a short time ago. The remains of the anti-gravitational disc still littered the area beneath the wrecked cowling, and they passed through the arch that the Daleks had cut in their own door. Rebec shuddered, remembering the nightmare journey up the chimney. Now they were back again The only difference was that they had a bomb—and the Doctor's plan.

The Doctor himself seemed cheerful and confident. 'See what you can find to make a barricade and seal off the end of that corridor,' he ordered. 'The Daleks are bound to arrive soon. We've got to delay them as long as we can.'

He ran up the ramp and looked through the hatch that gave on to the arsenal. His face clouded as he looked at the Daleks in their motionless ranks. Rebec came up the steps and joined him. She gasped at the sight of the Dalek army. 'The greatest Dalek invasion force ever assembled,' said the Doctor. 'Equipped with the Spiridons' power to become invisible. Nothing could stop them!' He slammed the hatch closed.

'Let's give the others a hand with that barricade.'

Taron and Codal had ripped up work-benches and shoved pieces of machinery into quite a formidable barrier. The Doctor and Rebec helped them to add the finishing touches.

All their lives depended on the strength of the final result.


In the control centre the Expedition Commander was listening to a report from his second-in-command. 'Message from Supreme Command space-craft. The Dalek Supreme will shortly arrive on Spiridon. He will assume total command of all operations on this planet.'

The Commander accepted the news without complaint. 'Understood. Continue.'

'Supreme Command have identified the alien who is not of Thal origin. He is the one known as the Doctor, the greatest enemy of the Daleks.'

The Commander considered. 'He will have much valuable knowledge. He must be captured and interrogated.'


Jo and Latep were still quite close to the Dalek city when they saw the little space-craft come into land. Sinister and saucer-like, it glided into an open space near the city entrance. Crouched at the edge of the jungle, Jo and Latep watched.

A ramp appeared silently from the body of the ship. A door opened and two Daleks glided down, taking up a position at the bottom, one either side. A third Dalek appeared at the top of the ramp. Its body-colour was not the usual silver but a gleaming black, and its dome shone brightly in gold. This Dalek glided smoothly down the ramp and set off towards the city, followed by the two aides.

Latep's voice was full of awe. 'That was the Dalek Supreme, head of the Supreme Council. Second only to the Emperor himself.'

Jo was staring thoughtfully at the spaceship. 'That doesn't look too different from your own craft. Could you fly it?'

Latep nodded. 'Any of us could. We've studied captured Dalek ships.'

'Then you could use it to get back to Skaro! Don't you see, you're not marooned here any more. I wish we could tell the others.'

'Maybe it's as well we can't.' Latep spoke seriously. 'There's something to be said for thinking you're on a suicide mission. You've got nothing to lose.'

Jo looked at him in exasperation. 'I thought you'd be pleased there was at least a hope of getting away.'

Latep smiled. 'Believe me, I am. I think I've found a very good reason for wanting to stay alive.' He looked directly at Jo as he spoke.

Jo turned quickly away. 'We'd better get moving again. There's still a long way to go.'

The Doctor stared at the machinery in the cooling chamber and cursed fluently in an obscure Martian dialect. Taron couldn't understand the words, but the meaning was plain enough. 'What's the matter, Doctor?'

'I was hoping to find a way to lock these controls in the "on" position. As soon as the refrigeration's switched off, the Dalek army is going to start coming to life. Won't work though, the main switches must be in the central control area. We'll have to use my other plan. Taron and Rebec, keep an eye on the barricade, Codal, you come with me.' He led Codal out into the corridor and used his sonic screwdriver to open the smaller door that led into the Dalek arsenal. Codal stopped short at the sight of the immense army of Daleks, but the Doctor said cheerfully, 'Don't worry, they're all fast asleep.' He pointed to a ramp leading up to the metal catwalks surrounding the huge cavern. 'We're going up on to those catwalks, Codal, you one way and me the other. We're looking for a nice large fissure in those walls...'

The Dalek Supreme, flanked by his aides, stood in central control. The area had been cleared. The Dalek Commander and his second-in-command stood before him. Harshly the Dalek Supreme addressed the second-in-command, ignoring the Expedition Commander. 'Report on invisibility experiments.'

'Daleks can achieve invisibility for two work periods only. In excess of this period, breakdown from light wave sickness occurs.'

'Satisfactory. The Supreme Council has ordered our army to be activated immediately. The invasion of the galaxy will begin at once. Close down refrigeration unit.'

'I obey.' The second-in-command moved away.

The Dalek Supreme turned his attention to the Expedition Commander. 'The action of hostile aliens has caused disruption of our operations on this planet.'

'The matter was beyond my control.' The Commander spoke without hope, knowing he was already condemned.

'Your orders were to exterminate them.'

'It has not been possible. Because of Spiridon sabotage we could not use the bacteria.'

The Dalek Supreme paused for a moment and then delivered judgement. 'The responsibility was yours. You have failed. The Supreme Council of the Daleks does not accept failure.'

The Expedition Commander stood quite still, accepting his fate. The guns of the Dalek Supreme and his aides blazed together, and the Commander exploded in smoke and flames.

Latep and Jo stood at the top of the chimney shaft. Latep had rigged up a kind of derrick made from tree branches gathered on the way. One end of an immense coil of rope was secured to it, and he was paying the other down into the shaft. Jo looked on full of misgiving. 'Suppose that contraption doesn't hold?'

Latep grinned. 'It'll hold.'

'Well, suppose the rope isn't long enough?'

'Jo, we've got every piece of rope in the entire

expedition fastened together. Believe me, it'll be long enough. Your friend the Doctor worked it out.'

Jo smiled wanly. 'It's not only the trip down that worries me: it's what we'll find at the bottom.'

Latep grinned encouragingly. 'We'll find the Doctor and the others, just as arranged. I'm off. Follow me when I call.' He swung his leg over the parapet, gripping the rope with his hands and feet.

Jo leaned forward and kissed him quickly on the cheek. 'Good luck, Latep.'

'And to you, Jo.' He slipped down out of sight. Jo waited anxiously until she heard his voice booming up the chimney. 'It's all right, Jo, come on.' She climbed the parapet, gripped the rope in the way he'd showed her and started following him down.

The Doctor was still searching when he heard Codal call, 'Doctor—I think I've found what you need.'

The Doctor ran along the catwalk to join him. Codal, the precious bomb at his feet, was standing by a jagged hole in the rock walls.

The Doctor examined it with interest. 'Now that looks promising. How deep is it?'

'Pretty deep I think, I can get my arm inside.' Codal demonstrated.

Taron appeared in the doorway of the arsenal. 'Doctor, the Daleks have reached the barricade—they're attacking it now! And the cooling unit seems to have been switched off. The temperature's rising.'

The Doctor paused. 'So it is. It'll only take a very

small rise for these Daleks to start moving. We've got to work fast, Codal.'

Codal wasn't listening. He was staring fascinatedly down into the arsenal itself, his eyes wide with horror. 'Look, Doctor.' He pointed. The Doctor looked. In the ranks of Daleks below him, gun-sticks were swivelling uncertainly, eye-stalks waving in unfocussed menace. Some of the Daleks were shifting a little, bumping gently against their neighbours. Sluggishly, reluctantly, but quite unmistakably, the army of Daleks had started to come to life.

# 12

# The Last Gamble

Taron and Rebec looked down the corridor from the cooling chamber towards the barricade at the far end. It was shuddering rhythmically as Daleks hurled themselves against it. At first they'd tried blasting it aside, but that had simply melted the metal and welded it together more strongly. Now they were using brute force, hurling themselves against it in relays like battering rams. It was a slow and clumsy method, but effective. Already parts of the barricade were beginning to fall away.

'A couple more tries and the whole lot will come down,' said Taron. 'Time we pulled back.'

They went through into the Dalek arsenal, and Taron touched the controls to close the door. There was no response. Taron shook his head. 'It's no good, the Daleks have cut off the power.' They climbed the ramp to the catwalk, joined the Doctor and Codal, who were busily enlarging their fissure by clearing out the rubble. 'The door won't shut, there's still no sign of Jo and Latep and the Daleks are nearly through the barricade,' reported Taron briskly. 'What now?'

The Doctor considered for a moment. 'They must have got all these Daleks *in* here somehow, and presumably they've provided a way to get them *out*. I don't suppose they're planning to take them up in the lifts, one by one! My guess is that one of these catwalks will lead to an exit, probably some sort of ramp. See what you can find.'

Taron and Rebec raced away, and the Doctor stretched a long arm inside the fissure. 'That seems to be clear enough. Pass me that bomb, Codal.'

Codal swung round to pick up the bomb—and caught it with the side of his foot as he turned. The bomb rolled slowly towards the edge of the catwalk. Codal dived for it, but just too late. Eluding his fingers by inches, the bomb rolled off the edge and fell to the area below.

The Doctor and Codal braced themselves—but nothing happened. Codal peered over the edge. 'There it is, down there.' He pointed. The bomb had rolled a few feet and lodged against the base of one of the Daleks. The Doctor looked. The drop was only about ten feet. Without hesitation he lowered himself over the edge, hung by his hands for a moment and dropped.

For a moment the Doctor stood still, gazing around him. Talk about Daniel in the lions' den, he thought. Here he was in full view of an entire Dalek army. The Daleks seemed dimly aware of his presence, but were still too dormant to do anything about it. Eyestalks swivelled slowly in an attempt to follow his progress as he picked his way between the stirring forms. Sucker-arms and gun-sticks waved erratically at him, and the slow-moving bodies of the Daleks jostled him as he walked. Working his way through the crowd of Daleks, the Doctor moved towards the bomb. The Dalek against which it was resting started moving too, and the bomb rolled further away, to be knocked further still by yet another Dalek. It was like a ghastly slow-motion football game, thought the Doctor, with thousands of players on the other side.

Dodging through the obstructing Daleks he reached the bomb at last and scooped it up. Codal was watching anxiously from the catwalk when the Doctor called 'Here!' and tossed him the bomb. With a gasp Codal caught it. The Doctor worked his way back to the catwalk. He jumped to swing himself up, but it was too high—he couldn't get a good enough run in the crowded space. The Daleks were pressing in on him now, as if trying to crush him. The Doctor climbed nimbly on top of the nearest Dalek and used it as a launch-pad for a flying leap to the catwalk. Codal was examining the bomb anxiously. 'I *think* it's all right, but the timing mechanism's damaged. It'll take me a few minutes to fix it.' He produced tools from his belt and got to work.

Taron and Rebec came running back along the catwalk. 'You were right, Doctor,' said Rebec excitedly. 'There's a huge spiral ramp over on the far side. It must lead right to the surface.'

'Excellent. That's our way out, when the time comes.'

'Isn't it about time you explained the rest of your plan?' asked Taron.

The Doctor smiled. 'I'm sorry—you've been very patient. Well, as you know, this arsenal is right on the edge of the icecano. The Daleks built it there deliberately so they could use its cooling power. This whole area is honeycombed with ice tunnels—and the icecano is unstable. If we explode our bomb in exactly the right place, it could make the icecano erupt *and* weaken the walls. The ice will break through and flood this entire cavern. That's the theory, anyway. We'll just have to hope it works.'

'The ice won't destroy them,' Rebec pointed out. 'It will just put them into suspended animation again.'

'With only one bomb that's the best we can hope for. Besides, once the chambers are flooded it will take centuries to seal off the icecano and get the Daleks out.'

The Doctor was interrupted by an explosion from outside the chamber. He turned to Codal. 'You'd better hurry, old chap. That sounded like the last of the barricade—they've used explosives!'

Back in the cooling chamber, a pair of legs appeared beneath the shattered cowling. Latep dropped to the ground, followed by Jo. He helped her up. 'You all right?'

'I think so,' she gasped. 'What's that noise?' From the corridor outside came a tremendous banging and clattering. They crept to the door and peered out. Daleks were pushing aside the remains of the shattered barricade. Jo looked anxiously at Latep. 'We've got to stop them!'

Latep unslung his bomb from its holder, made a quick adjustment to the timing mechanism. He stepped boldly into the corridor and bowled the bomb at the Daleks. A Dalek fired the moment he appeared.

Latep threw himself backwards, the blast missing him by inches. For a moment the gleaming cylinder sat harmlessly in the middle of the Daleks. Then it exploded, shattering the nearest Daleks and bringing down a pile of rubble that blocked off half the corridor.

Jo and Latep strained to see through the dust and smoke. At the far end of the corridor, Daleks were already beginning to push aside the rubble.

'They don't give up, do they?' said Jo. 'Let's go and find the Doctor.' They ran into the arsenal and along the catwalk. Rebec, Taron and the Doctor, still waiting for Codal to finish his repairs, greeted them enthusiastically. 'The Daleks are nearly here,' warned Jo. 'We used our bomb to try and stop them, but it didn't work.'

Codal looked up. 'All right, I've finished.'

The Doctor gave a sigh of relief. 'Taron, you lead the others to the surface. Codal and I will set the bomb and follow you. Codal, set the bomb to detonate in thirty seconds.'

Taron, Rebec, Latep and Jo ran along the catwalk towards the ramp.

The Doctor watched Codal touch a control on the bomb. 'Detonator running,' said Codal, and passed the bomb hurriedly to the Doctor. The Doctor thrust it deep inside the rock-fissure, groping to wedge it in a good position.

In the corridor, the Daleks pushed aside the last of the rubble and glided towards the arsenal door. The Doctor withdrew his arm from the fissure. 'Right, that should do it. Come on!' They started running along the catwalk, just as the first Daleks glided through the arsenal door. The Daleks moved cautiously up the ramp, and on to the catwalk.

The Doctor and Codal tore along the catwalk, leaving the Daleks behind. On the far side of the arsenal, the other four were waiting. Behind them a huge spiral ramp led upwards into darkness.

The little group anxiously watched the Daleks move slowly along the catwalk. The Doctor could hear Codal counting under his breath. 'Seven, six, five, four, three, two, one ...'

As the leading Dalek drew level with the fissure, the bomb exploded. There was a blast of flame and smoke from the fissure, and the Daleks were blown clear into the arsenal, crashing down upon the waking army. The catwalk was twisted and wrecked. For a moment it seemed that was all. 'It hasn't worked,' breathed Codal. 'They'll repair that damage in no time. We've failed.'

'Wait,' said the Doctor quietly. They heard a low rumbling. Cracks were appearing in the rock wall by the fissure, like the cracks made by dropping a stone on to thin ice. The cracks lengthened, spread ... Suddenly a whole section of wall burst inwards and a river of liquid ice began flooding through. The huge cavern was flooding as they watched. As the searing cold of the liquid ice rose around their bodies, the army of Daleks froze into immobility, resuming the long sleep from which they had so briefly awakened. From outside the arsenal came a threatening roar as ice broke through to other parts of the city. The icecano had erupted.

The Thals were already running up the spiral ramp. Jo tugged at the Doctor's sleeve. 'Come *on*, Doctor!'

The Doctor paused for a last look. The huge cavern was more than half-filled with ice by now, the helpless Daleks disappearing beneath the flood. '*Most* satisfactory,' said the Doctor with a smile. He and Jo ran after the others.

There were only three Daleks left in central control, the newly arrived Dalek Supreme, and his two aides. All members of the Dalek expedition to Spiridon had been involved in the final attempt to capture the Doctor, and were now trapped by the erupting ice.

The leading aide was calmly reading the instruments in the control room, relaying a story of unmitigated disaster. 'Arsenal and all lower levels inundated. Molten ice rising rapidly through all levels. No response from any Dalek unit.'

The Dalek Supreme spun round. A trickle of molten ice was flowing through the door of a central control. 'Advise Supreme Command. Attack force totally immobilised. No survivors. Set self-destruct on all instruments. We are abandoning.'


The Doctor and his friends were gathered round the ramp that led to the Dalek space-craft. Codal had opened the door with ease, and was happily checking the controls. They heard a low hum of power as the ship was readied for take-off. 'Time to go,' said the Doctor cheerfully.

Rebec was holding Taron's hand. 'And now we *can* go back home, to Skaro. That's something I never expected.'

Taron turned to the Doctor. 'There's no adequate way of thanking you, Doctor, but if there's ever anything we can do?'

Vastly embarrassed, the Doctor shook his head. Then he said, 'Wait, perhaps there is something. The Thals have always been a peace-loving people. I'd like to think they'll remain so. When you get back home, you'll be heroes. But don't glamorise your adventures. Don't make them think war is an exciting game. Tell them about the fear and the danger, the friends who won't be coming back.'

Taron nodded gravely. 'You can depend on us, Doctor. Good-bye.'

Taron and Rebec hurried into the ship. The Doctor looked for Latep and Jo, who had been talking a little apart from the others. They came up to him, Latep holding Jo's hand. He looked nervous but determined. 'I've been trying to persuade Jo to come back to Skaro with me, Doctor. Would you object?'

The Doctor looked down at Jo. 'Not if that's what she wants. Is it, Jo?'

Jo smiled tearfully at Latep. 'I'm sorry, Latep, I'm afraid it isn't. I like you very much—but I've got my own world and my own life to get back to.'

Latep nodded. He held out his hand. Jo shook it, then kissed him on the cheek. He hurried up the ramp.

Taron appeared in the doorway. 'You'll need these to get back into your ship, Doctor,' he called, and tossed down a plastic-wrapped bundle. 'Good-bye, and thanks again!' They heard a chorus of good-byes from inside the ship, then the door closed and the ramp retracted. Jo and the Doctor ran to the edge of the jungle, then turned to watch the take-off. With a roar of its booster-rockets the ship blasted-off, disappearing into the sky on its way back to Skaro.

The Doctor examined the bundle Taron had thrown him. It held two sets of the plastic protective clothing and a spray. 'Very thoughtful of him,' he said. 'We'd have had a job getting back in the TARDIS without these.'

Jo wasn't listening. She pointed to the blockhouse guarding the entrance to the Dalek city. From it were emerging the Dalek Supreme and his two aides. 'Oh dear,' said the Doctor. 'I don't suppose they'll be too happy about the Thals taking their spaceship.'

'No.' Jo smiled. 'I don't suppose they will.'

Jo and the Doctor turned and ran. A blast from a Dalek gun set fire to the jungle beside them. As they hurried through the undergrowth they heard the outraged voice of the Dalek Supreme, 'Aliens! Pursue and exterminate!'

Fortunately for Jo and the Doctor, the Dalek Supreme and his aides were strangers on Spiridon, and knew far less about the planet than they did themselves. It didn't take long to lose them in the dense jungle. After that, it was just a matter of enduring the long trek back to the point where the TARDIS had first landed.

When they reached the ruined temple it took them quite a while to recognise the TARDIS. The sponge-plants had been unable actually to *eat* it, but they'd covered it so thoroughly with their fungus that it looked rather like a large, square sponge. The Doctor and Jo put on the protective plastic garments and the Doctor sprayed TARDIS until he found the door. Once it was located, he concentrated on clearing the fungus with the spray so that he could open the door.

Jo looked on as he worked. The sponge-plants, aroused by their presence, were spitting angrily. Jo shuddered as she saw the white blobs spattering on the Doctor's plastic coat, remembering her own infection before she'd been cured by Wester. Poor Wester, he thought. The Doctor had told her of his self-sacrifice ...

Suddenly Jo saw three gleaming shapes approaching through the jungle. With incredible persistence, the Daleks had found them again.

She tapped the Doctor on the shoulder and pointed. The Doctor nodded unperturbed. 'Nearly done, Jo. The lock's bunged up with this stuff, and the key won't turn.'

The Doctor worked unhurriedly. The Daleks moved steadily closer.

'Hurry, Doctor,' said Jo. 'They'll spot us any minute now!'

She was right. Seconds later the leading Dalek registered the figures standing by the TARDIS. It fired at once, and the blast scorched a patch of fungus from the TARDIS's side. But the Doctor had the door open now. 'Hurry, Jo,' he yelled. Running past the gauntlet of the spitting sponges, Jo dashed inside, and the Doctor slammed the door behind them.

By now all three Daleks were approaching the TARDIS, gun sticks blazing. But they were too late. The TARDIS is invulnerable to outside attack. The Daleks watched helplessly as the TARDIS dematerialised, fragments of fungus dropping to the ground. Their greatest enemy had defeated their plans and escaped their vengeance once again.

The Dalek Supréme turned arrogantly to his aides. It had been a day of total catastrophe, the army buried, the Spiridon expedition wiped out, the city destroyed. Any other life-form would have been crushed by despair. But Daleks do not recognise defeat. They ignore it and carry on their chosen path of conquest and destruction.

There was utter confidence in the voice of the Dalek Supreme. 'Supreme Command will dispatch a rescue craft. Immediately on arrival, preparations will begin to free the army from the ice. We have been delayed, but not defeated.' The harsh voice rose triumphantly. *The Daleks are never defeated!*

Jo was feeding the protective garments into a disposal chute. 'Spiridon is one planet I *never* want to see again,' she said.

The Doctor finished his in-flight check, and moved to a monitor screen. He adjusted controls until the screen filled with stars, and then narrowed the focus down to one particular planet. 'What about this one, Jo?' he asked mischievously. 'That's Skaro. Any regrets?'

Jo smiled a little sadly, thinking of Latep's earnest

pleas. But she shook her head. 'No, Doctor. Skaro's not for me.'

The Doctor adjusted controls again. Another galaxy, and then another planet swam up on the screen.

'What about this little world?'

Jo looked at the planet floating peacefully in space. 'That's Earth, isn't it?'

The Doctor nodded.

'Then that's the one I want to see,' Jo said firmly. 'Home please, Doctor!'

The Doctor smiled. 'Very well, Jo. Home it is.'

He leaned over the control console and set the co-ordinates for Earth.